THAT'S HOW IT GOES

**A Novella By
Nick Ragone**

That's How It Goes

Copyright © 2024 by Nick Ragone

All rights reserved. This book or any portion thereof may not be reproduced, distributed, or transmitted in any form or by any means without the express written consent of the copyright holder, except in the case of brief quotations for the purpose of reviews and certain other noncommercial uses permitted by copyright law.

This is a work of fiction. Names, characters, places, and incidents are a product of the author's imagination or are used fictitiously. Any resemblance to actual people, living or dead, or to businesses companies, events, institutions, or locales is completely coincidental.

Dedicated to the extraordinary men and women of the Greatest Generation. Their selfless devotion to their country and each other will echo through all eternity.

Chapter 1

THE PREDAWN DARKNESS

PREDAWN DARKNESS SHROUDED the countryside as the roar of engines pierced the stillness. A C-47 transport plane hurtled down the runway, lifting into the moonless sky above southern England. The aircraft rumbled onward, dim lights barely illuminating the cramped interior.

Amidst the din, Robert Hickman took a deep breath, steadying his nerves. He was accustomed to the persistent roaring of the aircraft by now. The past few hours had passed in a haze—gearing up, boarding just after midnight, fruitlessly trying to catch a few minutes of sleep.

Robert gazed out the small window beside him. Far below, the inky abyss of the English Channel spread out, dotted by the outlines of waiting Allied ships. He steeled himself for the trials ahead as the drone of engines carried them toward their destination.

As he glanced around the plane, the other men in his stick seemed lost in their own worlds, girding themselves for what was to come. Their faces betrayed the emotions churning within. Fear. Excitement. Determination.

Robert caught glimpses of wide eyes, furrowed brows, nervous lip biting as the plane's interior lights swept by. These were mostly young men, many embarking on their first combat jump on this early morning. Sprinkled among them, Robert noted a handful of grim-faced veterans who had seen battle before. Their hands clutched rifles with casual familiarity.

Robert's own face revealed an unexpected calmness. At 20 years old, this would be his baptism by fire, but his jaw was set with resolve. He had trained for this moment for months, pushing his doubts aside. Now, with the French coast fast approaching in the dark hours of June 6th, 1944, he was ready.

The hum of the engines faded as Robert's mind drifted back to simpler times. He thought of his hometown in Connecticut and his time at Norwalk High.

***

November, 1941. Norwalk, Connecticut

Leaves of red, yellow, and orange carpeted the ground as he pedaled away from the red-brick school building.

As the final bell rang, students streamed out of the school and rushed toward buses, cars, and bikes.

Seventeen-year-old Robert coasted down the tree-lined neighborhood streets, passing the familiar shapes of neatly kept single-story houses. His was one of many working class families that called this place home.

Turning onto his street, Robert hopped off his bike and walked it up the front steps. He leaned the bicycle gently against the side of the house and went inside, ready for an evening of homework or listening to the radio. It was a simpler time, though the war raging in Europe rarely strayed far from people's minds.

As dusk fell, Robert emerged from his room at the sound of his mother, Doris, calling him for dinner. Doris Hickman was a sturdy woman in her early forties, with naturally wavy red hair she kept neatly pinned back. Though faint lines were starting to form on her pretty face after years of worry and hard work, her blue eyes still radiated kindness.

Robert sat down to pot roast, mashed potatoes, and green beans, one of his favorite home-cooked meals. After eating his fill, he cleared the table and fell into the familiar ritual of washing dishes alongside Doris.

Standing side by side at the sink, Robert handed each freshly cleaned plate to his mother. Her focus stayed fixed on the task of drying them, while Robert tried engaging her in conversation.

"Mr. Creighton in Social Studies said that it's only a matter of time before we're dragged into the war in Europe," Robert said, eager to discuss what he'd learned.

"Hmmmm ..." Doris responded absently, drying each plate.

Robert continued, urgency rising in his voice. "It's going to shi—shoot over there soon. Hitler controls the continent. If Britain falls, Creighton thinks we'll be next."

A lengthy, awkward silence followed, filled only by the clinking of dishes. Doris did not seem to register the gravity of her son's words.

"Mom, am I boring you? Are you listening?" Robert blurted in exasperation.

Doris continued drying the dishes, her lips pressed together in visible annoyance. She refused to look at her son as he persisted in trying to discuss the war.

"What do you want from me, Robert?" she finally said sharply, scrubbing the plate in her hands. "I'm not as worldly as your Mr. Creighton. Stop thinking about war and focus on college next year."

She paused, her voice softening. "It's the only thing your father ever wanted for you ..."

Doris's words trailed off as she stared distantly at the soapy dishwater in the sink, momentarily lost in bittersweet memories.

Robert stopped handing her clean plates. He moved closer and gently placed a reassuring hand on her shoulder, taking the plate from her hands and setting it aside. Doris seemed frozen in place, caught between past and present.

"I know, Ma," Robert said gently. "I'm going to college, I promise. But the world is changing. You heard President Roosevelt on the radio—they attacked one of our ships off Iceland. It's only a matter of time before they come for us."

Robert's voice dropped to a pained whisper. "If we go to war, I can't just sit in a classroom learning geometry and playing in the band when everyone else is enlisting ... I just can't. I'm sorry. I have to do my part."

He moved slowly back to the table to gather the remaining dishes, heavy-hearted but resolute.

***

The bell rang, jolting Robert from his thoughts. All around him students burst out of their seats, making a beeline for the classroom door. As the din of chatter and shuffling feet filled the room, Robert gathered his books unhurriedly.

He glimpsed Mr. Creighton at the front of the room, already erasing the day's lessons on "The Battle of Britain" and "Lend-Lease" from the blackboard. Robert felt a pang, wishing the discussion could continue. There was still so much to understand about the war in Europe.

Brushing past him, Robert overheard two students discussing the prospect of America entering the war.

"My old man says it's the Japs we have to worry about, not the Germans. They're tricky," said one boy.

"He says that 'cause you're German," scoffed his friend. "I don't see the Japs conquering Europe, genius."

Robert couldn't help but crack a wry half-smile. Everyone had an opinion, it seemed, though few understood the global forces at play. A familiar slender figure sidled up next to Robert, snapping him from his reflections.

It was Robert's friend Sal Variano, his dark tousled hair and soft face bearing an uncanny resemblance to a young Frank Sinatra. Sal's expressive eyebrows were already raised in anticipation of venting about the day's events. The two fell into easy conversation as they walked to Robert's locker.

Sal's voice took on an insistent, escalating urgency as he described the shame Benito Mussolini had brought upon his Italian immigrant family.

"My brothers *hate* Mussolini. Hate," Sal emphasized. "They're embarrassed ... I'm telling you, they might swim across the Atlantic and start fighting!" Sal insisted, only half-joking. "I'm not kidding!"

Robert looked at his friend with a mix of amusement and bemusement. Sal had a flair for dramatic pronouncements, but his frustration was real. If America entered the war, Robert knew Sal's family would be among the first in line to serve, eager to prove their loyalty.

Sal's agitation grew as he continued to rant about the injustices faced by Italian immigrants like his family.

"Tony is gonna enlist for sure. He says we all have to. He's tired of us being called greasy WOPs," Sal said, his voice rising. "Old Lady Dolman shot us a look at the market, like we support Mussolini! Can you believe that?"

Robert could see Sal getting increasingly worked up, as if trying to talk himself into the convictions he was professing.

"I'm gonna join the Army as soon as I turn eighteen. I don't care what my pop thinks. That'll show 'em. We ain't disloyal. I really am!" Sal insisted.

Reaching his locker, Robert calmly placed a hand on Sal's shoulder, hoping to ease his friend's fervor.

Opening the locker with his other hand, Robert empathized, "I know, I know. You're lucky that Tony is so gung-ho. I can't even discuss it with my mom ... It'll break her heart when I enlist. I'm the man of the house—I need to do my part."

Robert became lost in thought, staring blankly into the depths of his open locker.

"She wants me to stay twelve years old forever," he finally said somberly. "Maybe she thinks it'll bring my dad back."

Sal replied gently, "I mean, you're all she's got. Maybe just go to college. Nobody will hold it against you."

Robert slammed the locker door shut. "*I'll* hold it against me," he stated. His mind was made up, despite understanding the heartache it would cause his mother.

***

That following Sunday, Robert tagged along with Sal to the Variano household. From the sidewalk, Robert could glimpse activity stirring within the modest home.

Stepping inside, the scent of Carmela Variano's savory cooking filled the air. Sal's mother shuttled between the stove and dining room table as she prepared a feast for her bustling family.

Sal's little sisters, Maria and Izzy, were parked on the living room floor, listening intently to the radio playing a tune Robert recognized as "Chattanooga Choo Choo."

Meanwhile, Sal's father, Giuseppe, sat engrossed in an Italian newspaper, oblivious to the din.

Sal's boisterous older brothers held court in the corner, engaged in their typical spirited debate. "Fordham got crushed by Pittsburgh. Pittsburgh! Pitt's won three games all year! Stop with this *sciocchezze* about Fordham being better than Notre Dame," the broad-shouldered Tony insisted. Little Joe laughed heartily, defending Fordham's honor despite their recent drubbing by Pitt.

Robert watched the familial chaos unfold with amusement and envy. He had always loved the spirit of the Variano home, so unlike the subdued austerity of his own household. For better or worse, life with the Varianos was certainly never boring.

Little Joe laughed loudly, saying, "Seven Blocks of Granite? Remember them? We went to every game in 'thirty-six and 'thirty-seven. You were cheering louder than me! Have some loyalty."

The word "loyalty" triggered Tony; a look of anger flashed in his eyes,

"Loyalty?" he retorted. "Angelo Bertelli is the best quarterback in the country. He's one of us. And he plays for Notre Dame, not Fordham. Don't tell me about loyalty."

The brotherly bickering had been drowning out the music from the radio until Frank Sinatra's "I'll Never Smile Again" came on. The Variano sisters perked up instantly. "I can't hear Frank!" younger Izzy exclaimed, while she and her sister gazed adoringly at the radio.

"Nobody cares about stupid football!" Izzy added emphatically.

"Stop listening to that bum. He'd be nothing without Tommy Dorsey," Tony scoffed, referring to Sinatra.

Little Joe let out a loud guffaw. "What about loyalty? Isn't that bum one of us??" he retorted, catching Tony off guard.

Tony fumbled for a rebuttal to reconcile the clear hypocrisy. After a few seconds he managed a weak response. "He doesn't work for a living; he sings. He ain't gonna win no Heisman Trophy."

Sal was amused by the entire exchange. Mimicking Sinatra, he grabbed an imaginary microphone and crooned along passionately: "... for tears would fill my eyes, my heart would realize that our romance is through ..."

It was an unpolished but convincing rendition that held everyone's attention for a moment. Tony finally had enough. "Okay, *bello ragazzo*, that's enough," he said. "Go help your mother bring the food out."

Sal took a mock bow before heading to the kitchen. Robert stood awkwardly off to the side, trying his best not to be noticed amidst the familial chaos.

Tony waved dismissively towards the kitchen where Sal had gone to help his mother. "Talk some sense into lover boy," he said to Robert.

Robert just stared back blankly, unsure how to respond.

"World don't need more singers. We need fighters," Tony continued gravely. "We're about to go to war."

This got Robert's full attention. He slowly walked closer to Tony, eager to engage him on the pressing subject. "Our Social Studies teacher, Mr. Creighton—" he began.

But Tony cut him off, the words spilling out in frustration. "This Mussolini sickens me. We get called WOPs. No-Good, EYE-talians. People stare at us, like WE made a deal with Hitler. I'll be the first to go over there. And the rest of youz are going to."

"I'll be right behind you," Little Joe quickly agreed.

Robert thought he heard Sal mumble something in response as well, though it was hard to make out the Sinatra song still playing in Sal's head.

"I don't know what we're waiting for. We should just declare war on those bastards," Tony declared vehemently.

"Guarda che dici!" Carmela Variano suddenly exclaimed from the kitchen. Robert wasn't sure if she objected to Tony's use of the word "bastards" or his putdown of Mussolini.

"We should, Ma!" Tony yelled back unapologetically.

By now, the dining room table was fully set with Carmela's sumptuous cooking on display. The smells wafting from the kitchen made Robert's mouth water.

On the radio, the upbeat "Boogie Woogie Bugle Boy" by the Andrews Sisters came on, diverting the Variano sisters' attention. They hopped up from the floor as their father folded his newspaper and rose from his chair.

"Venite a mangiare, " Giuseppe declared, summoning everyone to the feast.

The family convened around the table and took their seats. Robert found himself at the far end next to Sal, with Giuseppe assuming his rightful place at the head.

As everyone bowed their heads for the customary Italian blessing, it took Robert a moment to recognize what was happening before he clumsily followed suit.

Giuseppe Variano bowed his head and began reciting the blessing in Italian. "Bless us, O Lord, and the food we are going to have," he said solemnly. "Let it not to lack to anyone anywhere in the world, especially to children."

After a brief pause, he enthusiastically concluded, "Mangiari!"

Carmela started serving the feast, beginning with her husband. "Dami il tuo piato," she directed Robert, indicating for him to hand over his plate.

As Tony began eating, he turned to Robert with a probing look. "So you a dreamer like Sal? Or you got your feet on the ground?"

Robert was caught slightly off guard by the question. "Um ... I ... I don't know," he stammered, glancing at Sal for help but finding none.

"I'm definitely no singer, if that's what you mean," Robert finally managed.

Tony pressed further. "No, funny guy, what's your plan?"

Now Robert was genuinely baffled. "Plan for what?"

"Plan for what?!?" Tony asked incredulously. "We know you can't sing. Can you fight?"

It took Robert a moment to realize what Tony was implying. "Yeah, I can fight," he stated firmly.

"Hickman. That's German, right?" Tony questioned.

"German is two Ns. We're English," Robert corrected, slightly annoyed at the assumption. "Wouldn't matter where I'm from, Tony. I'm American. If we go to war, I'm going to war."

Just then Sal quipped, "You mean if your mom lets you."

The comment drew giggles around the Variano dinner table. Robert felt his face flush pink with embarrassment. He turned to respond to Sal, but at that moment the radio stopped playing "Boogie Woogie Bugle Boy."

A hushed silence fell over the room as an urgent news bulletin suddenly came over the airwaves. "We interrupt this program for a special news bulletin from the United Press," the announcer declared gravely. "Flash: Washington. The White House announces Japanese attack on Pearl Harbor. President Roosevelt expected to address Congress tomorrow. Stay tuned for further developments, which will be broadcast immediately as received. All regular programming suspended."

Disbelief and shock registered on the faces of everyone seated around the dinner table. Even the steady ticking of the grandfather clock in the background seemed to fade away as the broadcaster detailed the unthinkable attack.

A stunned silence lingered in the room for what seemed like an eternity. "Che cos era cuello?" asked a confused Giuseppe Variano, unsure of what had just happened.

"We're at war," Tony responded softly, dazed and still trying to absorb the shocking news himself.

"Vieni di nuovo?" Giuseppe asked again, not comprehending.

"We're at war!" Tony repeated more emphatically, snapping out of his stupor. The weight of his words seemed to sink in for everyone seated around the dinner table.

***

On December 8th, 1941, crowds packed into darkened movie theaters across America, still reeling from the stunning news broadcast over radio airwaves the prior day: Pearl Harbor had been attacked.

As the haunting images of destruction and billowing black smoke flickered across movie screens, hushed audiences sat riveted. The grave voice of the newsreel narrator rang out:

"The U.S. Naval base at Pearl Harbor, Hawaii, was the scene of a devastating and unprovoked sneak attack by the Japanese forces in the early morning hours of December seventh. Their plan was straightforward: destroy the Pacific Fleet. Hundreds of fighter planes descended on the base without warning, where they damaged or destroyed nearly twenty American naval vessels, including eight battleships and over 300 airplanes. More than 2,400 Americans died in the attack, including civilians, and another 1,000 people were wounded. The attack took place at the exact same time the Japanese Ambassador was meeting with Secretary of State Hull to secure 'peace in the Pacific.'"

Footage showed the smoldering remains of the USS Arizona as it sank. Calcified bodies of sailors still manning anti-aircraft guns sat frozen in time.

As the Pearl Harbor images faded from the screen, a heavy silence lingered in the darkened theater. Shock, grief, and smoldering outrage mingled in the air. Sons, brothers, fathers, and friends would soon be called to war. The America that audiences had known and loved seemed to disappear in smoke along with the devastated Pacific Fleet.

***

Driving toward the market on that otherwise ordinary morning, Doris couldn't help but notice an unsettling quietness pervading the normally bustling streets. As shopkeepers raised metal gratings and unlocked doors, the customary chorus of lively chatter and activity felt muted.

Approaching the central marketplace near the docks, Doris slowed the car. Something else unusual caught her eye—a line of men snaking around the building of the Army recruitment center on 18th Street. Even at this early hour, the line stretched far longer than Doris had ever seen.

Pulling the car over, Doris parked across from the recruitment center and gazed at the solemn faces awaiting their turn to enlist. A tinge of dread crept over her as Robert's boyish visage flashed in her mind. Resting her head wearily on the steering wheel, Doris stared helplessly at the line of willing soldiers that was growing by the minute. Though it pained her to admit, she knew with chilling certainty that her beloved son would soon feel compelled to join them.

Chapter 2
Duty Calls

ROBERT FILED INTO Social Studies class alongside Sal, both noticing immediately that Mr. Creighton was absent from his usual position at the front of the room. In his place stood a tall, young, self-assured substitute teacher. Her confident posture and handsome, angular features commanded the room's attention.

"MISS DRURY" was neatly printed on the blackboard behind her. A conspicuous radio sat on the corner of her desk. Robert guessed it was there to provide any urgent war updates, though he hoped no news would interrupt class today.

"Settle in, please. I'll be teaching Social Studies today. My name is Miss Drury," the substitute announced after the bell rang.

"Where's Mr. Creighton?" blurted a curious student.

Miss Grace Drury's brows furrowed slightly in annoyance. "Hand, please. We raise our hands," she corrected firmly.

Looking chagrined, the student raised his hand. "Where's Mr. Creighton?" he asked properly this time.

"He's not with us today," Miss Drury replied matter-of-factly before continuing with class.

Robert felt unsettled by the teacher's absence so soon after the Pearl Harbor attack. Mr. Creighton's lessons suddenly seemed far away, part of a world that no longer existed.

The student blurted out "I can ..." before catching himself and remembering to raise his hand properly. "We can see that. Where is he?" he asked Miss Drury again.

"I'll be teaching this class for the time being. I've been told he's enlisted in the Navy," Miss Drury intoned without a trace of emotion.

A hush fell over the classroom at this news. The prior day's attack on Pearl Harbor suddenly felt very real and close to home with their own teacher leaving to serve.

"In a few minutes, President Roosevelt will be addressing Congress," Miss Drury continued. "I thought it important that we listen. Let's sit in silence while we wait."

Sitting in the back row, Robert and Sal slouched low at their desks, shields of notebooks raised to avoid notice.

Robert leaned over and whispered, "You think your brothers are gonna enlist?"

Sal whispered back, "Think? Tony and Joe were really worked up this morning, reading the papers. They start mixing Italian with English. Even got my pop lathered up."

Their hushed conversation was interrupted as Tommy Murphy leaned back from the row in front of them. Robert knew Tommy was one of the older students, already eighteen. His Boston accent was faint but noticeable.

"Your brothers work with my old man at the docks," Tommy whispered to Sal. "My mom just brought my lunch, and she said the whole waterfront enlisted today. It's a ghost town down there. She said she had to hold my old man back or he'd be gone too. Crazy old guy!"

"If my brothers join, then I gotta join," Sal whispered back earnestly. "I mean I want to. I'm not finishing school. I wasn't going to college anyway. I guess I'd rather fight than learn. I'll take over for Sinatra when I get back."

Robert chimed in quietly, "What about you, Murph?"

"I'm headed down to enlist today after school," Murph replied. "Turned eighteen three weeks ago. I'm gonna be a pilot. Pilots get all the girls."

Sal shot back, "That's good. 'Cause your face won't."

Undeterred, Murph retorted, "Hey Caruso, I didn't see you making time with anyone at Butler's dance. Guess your olive-oil charm took the night off."

"I don't need no charm. I got this," Sal insisted quietly. He then pantomimed singing dramatically, batting his eyes in an exaggerated swoon toward Miss Drury up at the front of the class.

Robert stifled a laugh. "If I didn't know any better, I'd think you're crooning to substitute pencil-up-her-ass," he whispered.

Sal just grinned wider. That's exactly what he was doing. "What can I say? She gives me the flutters," he declared. "Wait till I'm a big star—*she'll* be chasing *me*."

Lost in his crooner fantasy, Sal had forgotten to lower his voice. His antics caught Miss Drury's attention. "Quiet back there!" she admonished sharply.

The three boys quickly snapped to attention in feigned innocence.

"See, she has the flutters for me, too," Sal crowed triumphantly in an exaggerated whisper.

Robert and Tommy both rolled their eyes at Sal's delusions. Their friend was clearly smitten by this substitute teacher and the feelings were far from mutual.

"Hey, I didn't mean nothing about that crack about your mom not letting you enlist," Sal added, his tone turning serious. "I'm sor—"

But Robert cut him off. "Yes, you did," he said bluntly. "But I don't care. I said my piece to her. I can't be a kid forever. She can't just shield me from life. Once I'm eighteen she can't stop me from going."

At that moment, Miss Drury tuned the classroom radio, the signal fading in and out through static. Then the solemn, familiar voice of President Roosevelt suddenly rang out:

"Yesterday, December 7th, 1941, a date which will live in infamy, the United States of America was suddenly and deliberately attacked by naval and air forces of the Empire of Japan."

The classroom fell silent as all attention turned to the radio broadcast. Robert felt a mix of dread and resolve washing over him as the President detailed their country's entry into the war.

***

After school let out, Robert and Sal hurried to catch up with Tommy Murphy in the parking lot. He was already seated behind the wheel of his 1934 Plymouth PE DeLuxe, its throaty engine purring. As Tommy rolled down the window, the lively notes of "Little Brown Jug" could be heard playing on his radio.

"Hey, Red Baron, you going to enlist right now?" Sal called out, slightly out of breath from their sprint across the lot.

"You mean Eddie Rickenbacker?" Tommy chuckled in response. "And yeah, going to the one near the docks on Eighteenth Street."

Seized by excitement, Robert chimed in, "Can we tag along?"

Tommy eyed them doubtfully. "To enlist? Are you even eighteen?"

"Just to check it out," Robert clarified.

"I'm just going for the girls," Sal added cheekily. "Maybe I'll be a pilot like you."

Letting out an amused guffaw, Tommy waved them in. "Don't soil the seats, kids," he cautioned with mock gravity.

Eagerly, Robert and Sal clamored into Tommy's car, ready to witness the rush to serve at the recruitment center firsthand.

When they arrived, Robert was astonished to see the line of eager enlistees already snaked halfway around the block. After parking, the boys hustled across the busy street to take their place in the swelling queue.

Inside the bustling office, they could hear Dinah Shore's patriotic "Love that Boy" playing on the radio mingled with the energetic din. Recruiters in smart uniforms worked swiftly to process the new volunteers three at a time, but the flood showed no signs of abating.

Studying the faces of those around him, Robert noted many were athletic older men, not green youths like himself. Their determined expressions seemed to say the Japanese forces would soon face America's toughest on the battlefield.

"Man ..." Sal murmured under his breath, clearly intimidated by the brawny recruits surrounding them. "The Japs don't stand a chance ... We're sending over the Seven Blocks of Granite."

Broad-shouldered Tommy cast a skeptical glance at Sal's slender build compared to the older men. "We need to fatten you boys up," he remarked wryly. His own physique already boasted a sturdy mix of muscle and youthful bulk.

Moving nearer to the registration tables, Robert felt a simmering mix of anticipation and uncertainty. Events were already in motion far beyond his control.

As they inched closer, Tommy called out familiar names that he spotted in the line—Tommy O'Toole, Joey Sansone, the Manfriede brothers. "Oh and what's-his-name who dropped out in eighth grade," Tommy added. "I thought that guy died or something."

"Suozzo," Robert supplied. "Andy Suozzo. His old man went to jail ... boy, he got big." Robert spotted the hulking figure of their former classmate. "He might win the war by himself."

"Riiiight ..." Tommy chuckled. "The old guy worked on the docks with my dad. Family of thugs."

At last their turn came. The recruiter who greeted them was all business. Her no-nonsense expression and crisp uniform conveyed she was not to be trifled with.

"Okay, boys, take this form and begin filling it out," she instructed brusquely, handing them paperwork. "Don't leave any blanks." She eyed Sal and Robert dubiously before adding, "Once you're done with it you're going to ..."

Noticing Sal's youthful features, she interrupted herself to demand, "Hey, are you all eighteen?"

"I am, ma'am," Tommy replied politely, jabbing a thumb at his companions. "These two are still being potty trained."

The recruiter did not look amused by Tommy's joke. She stared back at them blankly. "Well, what are you doing here?" she demanded.

"We're getting ready for when we turn eighteen," Robert explained earnestly. "We wanna do our part."

For a fleeting moment, the hardness lifted from the recruiter's expression. The trace of a wry smile crossed her face. "Well, honey, you don't actually have to wait till you turn eighteen," she informed them. "You can enlist at seventeen with your parents' signature."

"Really?" Sal exclaimed in disbelief, elbowing Robert. They exchanged stunned looks, scarcely believing enlistment could come sooner than they realized.

"Yes, really," the recruiter confirmed crisply.

"Okay, ma'am, give us that form, please," Sal requested excitedly.

Back to business, the recruiter handed Sal and Robert the enlistment forms. "Take this, bring it home, get it signed, bring it back, serve your country," she directed them. Then gesturing to Tommy she added, "You take this form, go over there, fill it out, and come back to me. Now leave my line."

Clutching their precious forms, Robert and Sal staggered toward the recruitment office's front door in a daze, scarcely believing what had just transpired. The radio crooned Frank Sinatra's "That's How It Goes" in the background.

Just then, the boys nearly collided with none other than Miss Drury, their Social Studies substitute teacher. They all froze, stunned to encounter each other.

"Misses... Miss... um... " Robert stammered awkwardly, unable to recall her name. "What are you doing here?"

Quickly regaining her composure, Miss Drury straightened her posture and smoothed her blouse. "I could ask you two the same thing," she replied.

While Robert was still processing this chance meeting, Sal's initial shock transformed into an expression of doe-eyed delight. An enormous grin spread across his face.

"We're enlisting!" he proclaimed excitedly, waving the enlistment paperwork for emphasis. "Just need our parents' signatures. We're off to be heroes. Don't miss us too much when we're gone."

Miss Drury pressed her lips together, summoning all her composure not to smile at Sal's overt flirting. She seemed mostly amused, and perhaps a tiny bit flattered, too.

"Oh, I won't," she said dryly.

Eager to move past Sal's antics, Robert interjected, "What are you doing here? You teaching substitute Army today?"

Miss Drury's expression turned serious once more. "I'm enlisting," she said after a weighty pause. "I'm actually a registered nurse. Well, I have a nurse certificate from summering as a lifeguard. I got it back in St. Louis before I went to college."

Robert watched as she studied their faces intently while the significance of her words sank in. Her own face was somber. "There's a shortage of Army nurses," she told them. "We're in a shooting war now. This isn't the movies. Give it some thought before you rush off to be heroes."

Stung by her words, Robert retorted, "Hey, I know the score."

Miss Drury had gotten under his skin. "We're not in a classroom, and we don't need a lecture," he added defensively. "I'll get that at home tonight."

Sensing the growing tension, Sal tried lightening the mood. As "That's How It Goes" played on the recruitment office radio, he leaned into an imaginary microphone and sang along soulfully:

"That's how it goes, when you're in love with someone, and someone's not in love with you..."

Though Sal seemed to be crooning to an invisible audience, Robert kept his eyes fixed on his friend's face. Sal's singing was pitch-perfect and smooth as silk. For a moment, even the bustling room seemed to quiet down, drawn in by his golden voice.

Despite himself, Robert was impressed. Sal had deftly defused the awkwardness hanging in the air. They never saw Miss Drury's reaction before she hurried back into the enlistment line.

As the song ended, Sal beamed triumphantly. "Well, don't let them hurt that golden voice of yours," Miss Drury called over her shoulder sincerely. "Take care of yourselves over there."

The boys lingered, pondering the unexpected encounter with their teacher and her warning words. But with enlistment forms in hand, Robert felt his path was already set, for better or worse.

***

That evening, Robert lingered outside on the front steps of his house, anxiously turning the enlistment paperwork over in his hands. He had been summoned home for dinner, but hesitated to go inside, dreading the conversation ahead.

Finally, Robert took a deep breath and slowly pushed through the front door. Moving almost imperceptibly, he inched his way down the hall as his mother called out brightly from the kitchen, unaware of the document clenched in her son's fist.

"Robert, is that you?" Doris asked warmly. "I'm in here. Dinner's almost ready. I hope you didn't eat."

"Yeah, Mom," Robert answered haltingly. "Didn't eat. I'm hungry."

Entering the kitchen, he found Doris shuttling energetically between stove and table, tied up in an apron. The radio played a soothing instrumental version of "Sentimental Journey" in the background.

"Sit down. Pot roast," Doris directed him happily. "Oh, wait, can you get the milk?"

Robert slowly rose to get the milk from the refrigerator. Leaning against it heavily, he hesitantly began, "Mom ... Sal and I ... and Murph ... Tommy Murphy, we ... we went down to the docks, on Eighteenth Street."

He paused, head half inside the fridge. "We tagged along with Murph," Robert continued with difficulty. "He ... he went down there to enlist. He's eighteen."

Hearing this, Doris froze. The cheerful bustling ceased instantly, her hands gripping the back of the dinner chair for support. She knew where this was headed.

Seeing her reaction, Robert pushed on, willing himself to get the words out. "Sal and I ... they told us—"

But Doris cut him off, anger and fear rising in her voice. "Told you what?" she demanded. "What did they tell you down there? That you can enlist at seventeen? That you can enlist at seventeen with parental permission?"

Robert looked back astonished, as if she had been eavesdropping on them at the recruitment station.

"You don't think I'm aware of that?" Doris challenged, her jaw set defiantly. The paperwork clutched in Robert's hand felt like a hot coal singeing them both.

"I didn't ... No, I didn't. I ..." Robert stammered, struggling to find the right words.

Finally he spoke firmly. "You knew this was coming. Sal and I took the papers. His parents are signing them right now. His brothers have already enlisted. ... Murphy enlisted, too. Mr. Creighton's already gone. Heck, even our substitute teacher enlisted! She's not even a nurse, she was a lifeguard or something. They're all off to save the world!"

Seeing the crestfallen look on his mother's face, Robert's tone softened slightly. "I need you to sign mine too, Ma. I can't stay behind and let everyone else do the fighting."

Doris's eyes welled up with tears of anguish. A trickle streamed down her cheeks as reality sank in.

"I don't have to do anything!" Doris shot back angrily, defiance rising as a shield against the anguish in her heart. "I don't have to do *any*thing!"

As a mother, signing that paper meant relinquishing her sole remaining family to the mouth of war. Allowing her beloved only child to walk into the valley of death defied every maternal instinct she possessed. Her weary heart could not bear to let him go willingly, though deep down she knew Robert's mind was already made up.

No matter how tightly she had tried to hold onto her son's boyhood, Doris realized she could not stop the passage of time. Robert was determined to follow the call of duty, no matter the cost. Still, her soul railed against fate's cruel dictates and sought any way to protect her child from the brutal realities beyond Norwalk's borders.

"I'm going one way or the other!" Robert insisted ardently before catching himself. More gently he pleaded, "Please, Ma. Don't do this. Let me do my part. If you don't sign, it just means I'll go in March when I turn eighteen. Don't make me wait."

As the melancholy instrumental "It's Been a Long, Long Time" drifted from the radio, Robert slowly retrieved the enlistment paperwork from his back pocket. Holding it up with both hands, he gingerly inched it closer to his heartbroken mother.

Doris leaned in, the last of her resistance crumbling. They were both emotionally spent. Taking the paper from Robert's grasp, she collapsed against his chest, head resting over his heart. Robert wrapped his arms around her as she wept, gently stroking her hair.

Together they swayed slowly in a bittersweet dance, drawing strength from one another. Though they both knew this was the end of an era, tomorrow would dawn a new day. They had to meet it bravely, leaning on family ties that not even war could break.

THAT'S HOW IT GOES

Chapter 3

FAREWELLS

SAL STOOD AWKWARDLY on the familiar stoop of the Variano home, suitcase in hand, wearing an old suit of his father's that hung just slightly too large on his slender frame. Through the window he could glimpse the warm chaos of his family's living room one last time.

Suddenly, Carmela flung open the door and enveloped Sal in a fierce, crushing hug that made him squirm slightly. Though she tried to be stoic, Sal could hear soft sobs catching in his mother's throat as she clung to her son.

Over Carmela's shoulder, Sal glimpsed his teary-eyed little sisters hovering nearby. Giuseppe rested a supportive hand on Sal's back, gently nudging him toward the outside steps and the future that awaited beyond.

Stepping back, Carmela cupped Sal's face in her hands, drinking in his features as if trying to freeze this moment in her memory forever. Her eyes shone with a sorrowful pride that made Sal's heart clench.

With an emotional last wave, he turned and walked toward the waiting bus that would carry him away to war. Though his family's loving farewell warmed him, it could not completely banish the cold fingers of trepidation creeping down Sal's spine.

***

Robert gazed out the window of the speeding commuter train, watching the world fly by. The car was crammed with young men in civilian clothes eagerly chatting and laughing—new recruits on their way to training camp. Sitting with Tommy and Sal, Robert joined in the buoyant camaraderie.

When they stepped off at bustling Grand Central Station, the animated banter continued as they headed for the exit. Weaving through crowds of enlisted men with suitcases, they walked under the famous towering clock and out into the city.

Robert took in the scenes of soldiers embracing sweethearts, mothers waving tearful farewells, fathers clapping their sons proudly on the back. Though everyday commuters were few, an electric spirit of purpose and duty filled the terminal. It was all suddenly real—they were a small part of something far larger than themselves.

After the lively train adventure, Robert found himself filing into the frantic Army processing center in Times

Square alongside the other recruits. The nonstop energy of the city washed over him as they entered the massive facility.

Inside, they were herded into a crowded medical room filled with men in various states of undress. Nurses efficiently conducted physical exams at stations throughout the large space, with little privacy aside from thin partitions.

Robert stood nervously in a group of 12 men overseen by three no-nonsense nurses and a doctor. Nearby, Sal stepped up for his exam. Robert exchanged an awkward glance with Tommy as the nurse checked Sal's eyes, ears and throat with brisk precision.

"Open your mouth, say 'Ahh,'" she instructed. Sal obliged, but couldn't resist responding with a bit of awkward flirtatious banter, trying to lighten the uncomfortable situation.

As the nurse went to stick a tongue depressor in Sal's mouth, he hesitated. "Hey, be careful with that thing," Sal quipped lightly. "There's more gold in this throat than at Fort Knox."

His comment drew chuckles from Robert, Tommy and others within earshot. Obliging, the nurse pulled back the depressor. Sal theatrically cleared his throat and tried trilling a note, but instead emitted a frog-like croak. His mock look of grave concern elicited more laughter around him.

"Off with the shirt," the nurse instructed briskly.

Awkwardly, Sal removed his shirt to reveal an undersized, bony physique.

Eyeing his skinny frame, the nurse joked in exaggerated Italian-American accent, "Not much meat on these bones. Yo' mama no *mengiara*?"

Grinning playfully, Sal flexed his two scrawny biceps in response. "There might not be much, but what you see is choice cut!" he proclaimed gamely.

Watching Sal's clowning antics, Robert and the other recruits couldn't help but chuckle. Trust Sal to lighten even this uncomfortable situation, he thought with appreciation.

"I know you like what you see, nurse, but I'm spoken for," Sal continued smoothly. "Got me a girl back home. I mean a woman." He gestured voluptuously with his hands, as if tracing an invisible shapely figure. "Got me a woman back home," he added with a wink.

The nurse arched an exaggerated eyebrow as she went about examining Sal's breathing and heart rate. Robert tried not to smirk, knowing Sal was referring to Miss Drury, who was far from being "his girl."

From nearby, Robert heard Tommy jokingly call out, "Yeah, you might want to tell her that, Caruso."

"Put your shirt back on. Next up," the nurse instructed briskly, ignoring their antics.

As Sal and Tommy passed each other, Tommy grabbed Sal in an enthusiastic bear hug, squeezing a bit too hard as if to show off his superior brawn. The nurse didn't even glance up from her clipboard.

Watching Sal and Tommy, Robert felt a swell of camaraderie with his friends. But the looming reality of military service and the unknown future weighed heavily upon them all.

After finishing up with their medical exams, the recruits found themselves with some free time to explore New York City before shipping off to training camp the next day. As they emerged from the bustling Army processing center into Times Square, the lively tune of "Tuxedo Junction" caught Robert's ear.

He turned to see that the music was floating out from a nearby tourist shop. "Why are we here again?" Sal immediately questioned dubiously as they entered the crowded store.

"I want to get my mom something," Robert explained.

Misunderstanding his intention, Sal exclaimed incredulously, "We haven't been gone a day! How can you *possibly* be homesick already?"

Robert shook his head. "Nooo. I want to get my mom something," he clarified. "We've lived our entire lives in Norwalk, and she's been to New York City exactly once. Once. My dad took us to Yankee Stadium when I was ten to see Babe Ruth's final game with the Yankees. ... She never even made it into Manhattan."

Robert continued solemnly, "We ship out tomorrow. Who knows the next time we'll be in Manhattan."

As the others fanned out exploring, Robert methodically scanned the aisles, seeking the perfect gift. Unbeknownst to him, a cute salesgirl, about 19 years old, began discreetly shadowing his steps.

Robert was so engrossed in his search that the salesgirl's voice made him jump slightly. "Can I help you with something?" she asked politely.

He turned to see an approachable blonde girl gazing at him with friendly interest. "Um, no. I mean yes. Yes, I can use some help. I'm looking for a gift," Robert explained, recovering his composure.

"For your girlfriend?" the salesgirl inquired.

"No. No. For my mom. My mom. No girlfriend. My mom ..." Robert stumbled over his words, feeling his face grow warm.

He thought he saw mild relief flit across her face before her expression shifted to amusement at his flustered reply.

"Well, what does your mother-not-girlfriend like?" she asked playfully.

Robert gave an exaggerated eye roll. "My *moootthheeer* likes ..." he began before trailing off. He actually had no idea what gift his mom might want.

Sensing his dilemma, the salesgirl interjected teasingly, "Come again? Didn't catch that. She likes what?"

"I dunno. I have no idea," Robert conceded with mock exasperation. "I'm headed out to basic training tomorrow, and I want to get her something. Just help me, please."

"Happy to!" she replied brightly. As they browsed, she held up an elegant blue velvet cloche hat adorned with feathers. "We have some beautiful hats over here if you want to impress her," she suggested.

Robert looked back incredulously, unable to picture his mother wearing something so extravagant. As they continued walking, the salesgirl pointed out a display of vintage New York City maps. "Very popular with the tourists," she explained enthusiastically.

Shooting her an incredulous look, Robert corrected, "I'm not a tourist. We live a train ride away in Norwalk."

Realizing how unconvincing that sounded, he quickly fibbed, "We get into the city often."

"Oh, like to take in Broadway shows and go to fancy restaurants?" the salesgirl asked, a skeptical note in her voice.

Robert mumbled indistinctly, covering his mouth in embarrassment. "Yeah ..." he finally conceded, before admitting, "no ... we came here once for a baseball game."

"Okay, big spender. On a budget," she teased, suggesting a postcard instead. "I'm sure she'd love to hear from you. We have the Empire State Building, Times Square, Statue of Liberty; take your pick."

"Dunno ..." Robert murmured, still not finding anything that felt quite right. As he wandered the aisles, a display of souvenir pens caught his eye. He walked over to examine them more closely, the salesgirl following.

"*Excellent* taste," she approved enthusiastically. "Veeeerrry popular with the mother-not-girlfriends."

Robert's face lit up as he spotted one engraved with a miniature Empire State Building. "I'll be writing home a lot. This Empire State Building pen is perfect," he declared. "I'll take two—one for her, one for me."

"It has red ink, you know," she pointed out.

"Even better. Easier to read," Robert replied.

Her expression softened as it dawned on her what a thoughtful son he was. She quickly rang up the purchase, visibly touched by the gesture.

As they walked toward the register, Robert slowed his pace. "I'm Robert, by the way. Robert Hickman," he introduced himself, hoping to continue the conversation.

"Well, pleasure to meet you, Robert Hickman from Norwalk, Connecticut, and frequent New York City visitor with mother-not-girlfriend," she replied playfully. "I'm Peggy Carrol."

Robert's face lit up again. "That's my mom's middle name, Carol!" he exclaimed.

"I'm two Rs, silly," Peggy corrected him with a grin.

Emboldened, Robert asked hopefully, "I don't report to basic training until tomorrow. Are you free tonight?"

Peggy's face lit up. "Ever been ice skating?"

Later that evening, Robert found himself lacing up skates beside Peggy at the picturesque ice rink outside Rockefeller Center. Twinkling string lights and an enormous Christmas tree towered overhead, while the notes of "Moonlight Serenade" floated melodically from speakers.

All around, elegant couples glided gracefully across the gleaming ice. Their languid movements and easy smiles spoke of countless blissful evenings spent swirling across this urban oasis. Nearby, excited children teetered on their blades, while parents hovered protectively.

Surrounded by such effortless artistry, Robert felt utterly out of his element and clung awkwardly to the wall. The cold night air nipped at his exposed ears and fingertips. Watching others zip past, he tightened his borrowed gloves self-consciously.

"Why do I feel like I've been set up?" he joked to Peggy. "You must have known I've never been on the ice. What gave me away?"

"No scars on your face, all your teeth," she teased. "Too pretty to be one of those hockey players."

Robert had to laugh. "Well, I'm at your mercy," he confessed. "Just how you planned it."

Though unsure on his feet, with Peggy's occasional steadying hand, Robert felt lighter than he had in weeks.

Robert gingerly skate-walked, clinging to the wall for balance as graceful couples swooshed effortlessly past.

"Where are you from to be such a natural?" he asked Peggy, trying to make conversation.

"I'm from Yonkers but self-taught, here at this rink," she explained. "I've been coming since it opened in 'thirty-six. It helps me clear my head sometimes."

"Ah, I see. You bring *all* your male admirers here. Home rink advantage," Robert joked. "Makes sense."

He got a faint chuckle from Peggy. "You're the first, actually," she said, a tinge of wistfulness in her voice.

Just then, Robert slipped slightly. Peggy swiftly hooked her arm through his, keeping him upright. They stayed locked together as they continued skating.

"I don't really get out much," Peggy confessed quietly after a pause. Robert thought she seemed on the verge of saying more, but instead she changed the subject.

"Your dad must be very proud of you. You didn't waste any time to defend our country," Peggy remarked brightly.

Robert hesitated before answering. "My dad died when I was twelve," he shared. "He was a commercial fisherman. It was an accident of some kind."

They glided to a stop, arms still interlinked. Peggy looked stricken, not having expected such a somber reply.

"I ... I'm ... I'm sorry. I didn't mean to—" Peggy stammered.

"It's okay," Robert said gently. After a weighty pause, he continued haltingly, "It's not something I talk about much. But there's not a day that goes by when I don't think about him."

A thoughtful silence followed before Robert went on. "So it's me and my mom now. Who's now the proud owner of a fancy new pen," he concluded, mustering a faint chuckle to lighten the somber mood.

Robert took both of Peggy's hands sincerely. "Thank you ... for the skate. For listening. For spending time with this lonely and confused tourist," he said, a wry but grateful smile crossing his face.

His expression turned serious, almost confessional. "I insisted my mom sign the form so I could enlist before I turned eighteen ... She didn't want to. She really didn't want to. But she did. And now I think of her being by herself."

Robert paused reflectively before adding, "But I have to do my part. I hope I did the right thing."

Their hands remained clasped as they continued talking, the bustling rink fading away around them.

***

As the boys dispersed across the country to begin their military training, the folks back home settled into changed realities of their own. Daily life continued, but each person's reality was altered in small ways by lingering thoughts of their absent loved ones.

Aboard a southbound train, Tommy confidently shot dice with a circle of fellow recruits, wagers flying as the railcars rumbled along. On the periphery, Sal cheered Tommy on enthusiastically, though he lacked the funds to join the rowdy game.

Leaning against a grimy bus window, Robert watched the dusty Midwest landscape race by in a featureless blur. He found himself lost in thought, imagining the weeks of grueling training ahead and dangers unknown.

Gliding across the ice, Peggy smiled as couples swooshed gracefully past her at the Rockefeller Center rink. Despite the hubbub of happy families, she felt pangs of loneliness creep in as Robert's boyish face appeared unbidden in her mind.

Sitting alone at her too-quiet kitchen table, Doris picked at her lavish dinner spread to no avail. Nearby, the red ink of Robert's letter seemed to taunt her. She read his loving words again and again, praying nightly for his safe return.

Clad in a sleeveless olive drab T-shirt that revealed his prominent tattoos, Tony Variano held court among fellow trainees, boasting of past exploits back home. The gregarious older brother of Sal, Tony had always been quick to regale others with amusing and likely exaggerated tales of life in Connecticut. With his customary charisma, he now captivated his barracks mates, temporarily distracting them from the sobering training ahead.

Crisp in her new nurse's uniform, Miss Drury keenly shadowed the seasoned instructor's rounds at a busy hospital ward. She felt eager to put her training into practice, hoping to soon be saving lives rather than merely watching.

Crowded into their usual pew, what remained of the Variano family bowed their heads reverently in prayer. In spite of the familiar comfort of Mass, their thoughts strayed anxiously to their boys headed into harm's way.

Chapter 4

TURNING TIDE

ON A BALMY SATURDAY in late spring 1942, movie theaters were again packed with attentive audiences awaiting the latest weekly newsreel. As additional Pearl Harbor footage had shaken Americans from their isolationist slumber, these gripping updates from the front lines had become vital communal touchpoints.

The somber narrator's voice filled the darkened theaters as blurry images from distant Pacific battles illuminated the screens. "With British forces suffering defeats in Hong Kong, Borneo, Malaysia and Singapore, as well as Dutch losses at Sumatra and Java, the Japanese empire had its sights on an invasion of Australia," he intoned ominously.

The mood shifted as the narrator declared, "America is on the move in the Pacific! In the Coral Sea, America's naval might stopped the Japanese advance on Port Moresby in Papua New Guinea, halting their southern expansion and plans to invade northern Australia."

The audience exhaled in relief and swelled with pride at the turning tide. "The Imperial Japanese Navy's losses would factor into their resounding defeat the following month at Midway," the narrator continued.

Triumphantly he concluded, "No less than Admiral Nimitz himself called our stunning naval victory against the Jap invasion force at strategic Midway Island 'the greatest in naval history.' Eighteen Japanese ships, including four aircraft carriers, were either crippled or sent to their watery graves."

As the screens faded to black in preparation for the main attraction, spirits were buoyed by the first tangible news of American victory against the formidable foe that had ravaged Pearl Harbor just months prior.

***

Months passed by. Lying on his neatly made bunk in the crowded barracks, Robert closely read Peggy's latest letter, its pages soft and creased from frequent re-reading. He tuned out the idle chatter and occasional shouts echoing around him, focused only on Peggy's graceful handwriting as he devoured every word written just for him.

The other recruits constantly exchanged dog-eared photos and bragged of conquests back home, but Robert kept his treasured letters private. Curled in his corner bunk at the shadowy barracks' edge, Robert felt the rest of the room fall away as he read Peggy's neatly penned pages once more.

Outside, night was falling on his Arkansas training base, but Robert was miles away. He could almost imagine himself sitting beside Peggy, quietly listening as she revealed her innermost hopes and fears. He lingered over each line, knowing how much courage it had taken for her to open up so candidly through ink alone.

> I never thought running to the mailbox would be the highlight of my week, but it is. I measure time by when I receive your letters. I hope you do the same. Your letters always seem to come on Saturday. The girls at work say I'm in a noticeably better mood late in the week, which is probably true. I confess that I'm relieved that you had extended basic training and now additional training.
>
> Whatever plans they have for you—and I know you can't tell me—it must be an awesome responsibility. Maybe even dangerous. Every day in the paper we read about boys who won't be coming home, and it's heartbreaking. My friend Sally lost her husband in the Coral Sea. No body was even recovered. But knowing that you're still stateside gives me relief. I'm sure it does for your mom as well. I can only imagine how she feels seeing your letters, written in that beautiful red ink. Thank God some artful salesgirl convinced you to buy a magic pen!
>
> Every letter I want to tell you something and every letter I chicken out. I tell myself: next letter. Or in one of our phone calls. But you have leave in two weeks,

and I know I'll be seeing you. I'm six months pregnant. I had just found out days before we met and was still in denial, I think. I thought about telling you, but I was afraid it would scare you off. And I still am now. The father isn't in the picture. He never really was. He doesn't want anything to do with me or us. And that's fine with me. My parents have all but disowned me. I've been staying with my aunt in the Bronx. She has the patience of an angel and the heart of a saint. Life is complicated, but I'm not daunted. I've stopped feeling sorry for myself. I'll figure out what's best for us. I pray that it includes you, but I understand if it doesn't.

   Love, Your Peggy

Robert slowly refolded the pages and pressed them to his chest, breathing deeply. His mind swirled with possibilities about how Peggy's news might reshape their future.

He felt overwhelmed but resolved not to let fear guide him. The war had imparted painful lessons about embracing the gift of each day, come what may.

Robert knew that Peggy awaited his reaction during upcoming leave with equal parts hope and dread. He silently vowed that no matter what challenges awaited, they would face them together from now on.

Letting his head sink back onto the lumpy pillow, Robert tucked Peggy's treasured letter safely away as the raucous barracks chatter surrounded him once more. He said a tired prayer of thanks for having someone to dream of amidst the demanding uncertainty of training routines.

Robert drifted off to sleep, already composing his next letter to Peggy in his mind. No matter what lay ahead, their story was still being written. He clung to that certainty like a lifeline, allowing him to face the looming future without fear.

***

The sweltering Alabama sun beat down on Tommy Murphy as he stood on the edge of the bustling Maxwell Field tarmac, squinting against the glare. Nearby, military brass studied their clipboards with grave focus, scrutinizing every plane's takeoff and landing as they determined each pilot's future.

Tommy watched the small trainers ascend and sweep back onto the runway, envying the lucky few who would advance to flight school. The ambitious teen had joined up to become a pilot like his hero Eddie Rickenbacker, not toil in the infantry.

As another plane wobbled unsteadily on its landing approach, Tommy watched the pilot intently, knowing any minor mistakes could dash flight school dreams in an instant. He was determined to prove his worth in the cockpit no matter the challenge.

Later in the noisy mess hall, tensions ran high among the worn-out trainees. As they ate, a wisecrack from cocky Brooklynite Larry Manetti cut through the din.

"I hope I can hold down the slop they're serving today," Manetti grumbled loudly. "My stomach is still at 10,000 feet, thanks to Caruso."

He jerked a thumb toward Sal seated a few spots away. "It's a miracle we're still in one piece. This guy is jumpier than my girl when I get her alone." His crass joke elicited some laughs nearby.

"Do us a favor and stay on the ground, *paesano*," Manetti added, smirking.

Tommy glanced over at Sal, who sat hunched over his tray, avoiding eye contact. Though Larry's swaggering arrogance was grinding on Tommy's last nerve, Sal seemed unwilling to stand up for himself. Tommy stayed seated for the moment, holding his tongue. But Larry had no idea he was treading into dangerous territory by targeting his close friend Sal.

"I'm putting in a request for a new partner. I'm not washing out on account of this *gidrul*," Larry added derisively.

Tommy had finally heard enough. "You don't need Sal to wash you out, you can do that all on your own, *paesano*," he shot back, exaggerating the Italian pronunciation mockingly.

Larry turned, disbelief etched on his face. "What's that?"

"You heard me," Tommy continued, urgency rising in his voice. "This isn't some street corner in Brooklyn. Nobody gives a crap what you think, Man-yetti."

A hushed silence abruptly fell over the babbling mess hall.

Larry's face twisted furiously at the unexpected confrontation. "Oh, I see, coming to the defense of your girlfriend," he sneered. "What valor. You're gonna make a great grunt when you wash out, potato head."

At that, Tommy impulsively flipped his tray of food at Larry and lunged forward. It took four men, including an embarrassed Sal, to hold him back as Larry goaded him further.

"Let the tough guy go! Let the tough guy go!" Larry shouted animatedly. "I'll kick potato head's ass back to Ireland ... let 'im go!"

With a surge of adrenaline, Tommy easily shook off the men trying to restrain him. Seeing Tommy break free, apprehension flashed across Larry's face. But before punches could fly, two officers intervened, diffusing the close call.

As he stood down, Tommy had no idea whether he would face discipline for his actions. But given another chance, he would readily confront Larry again to defend his outmatched friend.

Later that afternoon in the officers' lounge, a group of senior officers leisurely sipped cocktails while reviewing the trainees' progress reports.

A mustachioed major in the corner asked about each candidate in turn. "Bader?"

"Yes," replied a freckled young lieutenant eagerly, giving a thumbs-up gesture.

A slender captain by the window paused briefly before also signaling his approval.

When they reached "Brophy," however, the major and two seasoned colonels decisively gave a thumbs down.

The bald colonel then asked the group, "Were any of you in mess at 1300 hours today?" The others shook their heads no.

"Why?" asked the major, his bushy white eyebrows furrowing with interest.

"The big Irish kid, what's-his-name, nearly took the place apart," the bald colonel explained. "Went after that wise guy. Kid is a really good pilot; what's his name?"

Glancing at his notes, the major supplied, "Murphy? Thomas Murphy."

The others nodded, familiar with the dramatic mess hall incident earlier that day.

"Right, Murphy. The old man wants me to discipline him, maybe bounce him from the program," related the bald colonel, pointing up toward their commanding officer's office overhead.

"I'm not. He's our best pilot," the colonel continued. "He was defending that skinny kid, the singer ... a mediocre pilot."

The slender captain by the window chimed in, "This Murphy looks like a meathead, but let me tell you, he can handle the stick up there. And we don't have a lot of them who I trust with a crew. ... I'm sure the hood had it coming."

"I suggest we keep Murphy, bounce the hood to gunner and the singer to navigation," proposed the mustachioed major decisively.

The others in the lounge all nodded in agreement at this solution for disciplining those involved without losing their top aviator recruit.

***

In the fading light of dusk, Doris settled into the lackluster armchair that she always occupied for her letter-reading ritual. Unfolding the creased pages covered in Robert's familiar neat script, she drew a shaky breath before diving in.

As her eyes devoured each line written just for her in vivid red ink, the chronic knot of worry in Doris's chest loosened slightly. She could hear her son's voice in the thoughtful words that transported her from the lonely living room to wherever he was in that moment.

Robert's descriptions of training were light on details, but rich with reassuring humor and optimism. He portrayed his fellow recruits as mischievous brothers, bonding under the watchful eye of tough but fair drill sergeants.

Reaching the last paragraph in which Robert sent his boundless love and urged her not to worry, Doris exhaled fully for what felt like the first time in weeks. Carefully refolding the worn pages, she sat back in the chair and smiled peacefully.

Tomorrow would bring new anxieties, but right now Doris allowed herself to bask in this connection with her beloved son. No matter the miles between them, Robert was always near when she held his letters close.

On his brief military leave, Robert gazed out the smudged train window, thinking of his mother back home as bare trees and scattered homes raced past. He pictured Doris settling into her armchair each night, unfolding his letters with shaky hands.

Across from Robert, Peggy sat cradling her belly, a tired smile on her lips. They leaned inward toward each other in easy familiarity.

When the conductor appeared, he offered a knowing smile while accepting Robert's ticket. His eyes twinkled with congratulations toward the young expectant couple.

As the conductor moved on, Robert closed the gap to clasp Peggy's hands in his with a gentle squeeze. Though uncertainty still swirled in both their minds, he continued conversing with her in hushed, optimistic tones.

Their interlaced fingers spoke of an unbreakable bond, despite the unexpected detour life had placed before them. Gazing into Peggy's tired but radiant face, Robert vowed to himself that he would do right by her and the baby, no matter what lay ahead.

Murphy stood chatting with Sal outside the barracks, trying to boost his dejected friend's spirits after being cut from flight school. Nearby, lines of buses idled, waiting to transport the washed-out cadets to new assignments.

Larry Manetti trudged past, shoulders slumped under the weight of his crushed dreams. His swaggering arrogance had vanished along with his pilot ambitions. Murphy couldn't resist flashing a satisfied smirk at his former nemesis' downfall.

Turning back to Sal, Murphy enveloped him in an affectionate bear hug, lifting the slender young man off his feet. "Keep your chin up, pal," Murphy said warmly as he set him down. "You'll make one heck of a navigator."

Sal gave a half-hearted smile in return. He would miss flying with his friend, but knew their paths were diverging. As he loaded his duffel bag onto an idling bus, Sal turned and caught Murphy's eye one last time. Despite their shared disappointment, Sal's expression glowed with gratitude for his loyal friend who'd stood up for him.

Murphy waved until the bus disappeared down the tree-lined road, hoping their fortunes would cross again when war flung them into action abroad.

Robert stood frozen on the front steps of his childhood home, Peggy's arm tucked in his. They exchanged an anxious look, both dreading Doris's reaction to their unexpected news.

"It'll be okay," Robert whispered, squeezing Peggy's hand reassuringly before finally ringing the bell. They heard footsteps rapidly approaching before the door flung open.

Doris's delighted smile at seeing her son quickly morphed into shock as she registered Peggy's rounded belly. Without a word, she turned and hurried back inside.

Exchanging pained expressions, Robert and Peggy hurried after her. Entering the house, Robert called, "Mom, wait up!" as he closed the door behind them.

But Doris was already out of sight, having beat a hasty path to the sanctuary of her kitchen. Trailing breathlessly, the young couple braced themselves to shatter her illusion of her son's innocent youth once and for all.

Bursting into the kitchen, Robert saw his mother already seated rigidly at the table laden with food, staring straight ahead. Peggy hovered awkwardly nearby, still clad in her coat and hat.

"Slow down, Mom, we're out of breath," Robert implored. Seeing Peggy's discomfort, he gently took her coat and hat. As he stepped out to hang them up, Peggy stood alone under his mother's silent scrutiny.

Returning swiftly, Robert pulled out a chair for Peggy and helped her get seated. Turning to his mother, he jestfully remarked, "It's good to see you too, Mom. I see you've had a chance to spend time with Peggy." His lame quip fell flat in the tense air.

Awkwardly placing a souvenir Statue of Liberty pen on the table, he added, "Peggy and I brought you something ... a gift. A new pen from her store. Same beautiful, red ink."

Doris simply sat frozen, hands folded tightly in her lap, refusing to meet their eyes. Robert could see her biting her lip, holding back a torrent of confused emotions.

Trying to break the painful silence, Peggy spoke up graciously. "It's a pleasure to meet you, Mrs. Hickman. Robert has told me so much about you, I feel as if I know you already."

This was the opening his mother needed. "Well, I *thought* I knew you too," Doris shot back. "Clearly, I don't. It seems like some details were missing from Robert's letters."

"Mom, I can explain—" Robert began hastily.

But Peggy jumped in, hoping to absorb Doris's anger. "It was my decision to keep this from you, Mrs. Hickman, not Robert's," she explained gently. "I didn't think it was fair for him to burden you with my situation."

The word "my" caught Doris's full attention. For the first time, she turned to look directly at Peggy.

"I became pregnant before I ever met Robert," Peggy confessed. "The day we met, I knew. And for months I couldn't find the courage to tell him. I was afraid of losing him. And I wouldn't have blamed him. He has enough on his mind. I didn't want to be a burden. And I still don't want to be."

As she listened, some of the confusion and anger receded from Doris's face. She studied Peggy with new understanding dawning in her eyes.

"I wasn't sure about coming here today," Peggy added softly. "I'm sorry you had to learn about me this way."

Doris asked haltingly, "What ... I mean, how ... did ... what happened?"

"Wrong person. Bad decision. He's not in my life ..." Peggy replied simply. "But we don't get any do-overs."

Doris sat silent, a cocktail of emotions playing across her face—residual anger, confusion, mild sympathy bordering on pity. She clearly didn't know how to react to this revelation. The lavish meal sat untouched before them.

After a few tense moments of silence, Robert abruptly announced, "Mom ... Peggy and I are getting married. Tomorrow."

Both Doris and Peggy looked back in astonishment—this was news to Peggy too. Robert may have impulsively decided it on the spot.

"At City Hall," Robert continued earnestly. "We really want you to be there."

A heavy silence followed, filled only by the ticking of the kitchen clock. It was more than Doris could take. "You'll have to excuse me," she muttered hurriedly. "I need to get some fresh air." She bolted from the table without another word.

Robert and Peggy sat staring at their untouched plates, still stunned by Robert's spur-of-the-moment proposal.

Doris sat motionless on a weathered park bench, blindly staring ahead. The revelations from dinner swirled ceaselessly through her mind. She scarcely noticed when Peggy approached and lowered herself gingerly beside her.

After several silent moments, Peggy finally spoke up timidly. "Robert told me you might be in the park, that you come here to clear your head sometimes."

Doris gave no reply, keeping her gaze fixed straight ahead.

Peggy continued gently, "I know the feeling. I have someplace like this, to clear my head."

At this, Doris slowly turned to look the girl in the face for the first time. "You don't know what I'm feeling," she said bluntly.

"You're right. I don't," Peggy acknowledged. "But I know what I'm feeling. I'm feeling like a burden to your son."

Peggy went on, "He's passed out on your couch. He's exhausted. Whatever he's training for, it's breaking him physically and mentally. He's aged five years in five months. Maybe it's my fault. Maybe it's the Army. Maybe it's the thought of breaking your heart. I can't imagine the stress he's under."

She paused, gently rubbing her protruding belly before adding, "Well, maybe a little."

Peggy's voice took on an urgent tone. "I know Robert won't be stateside forever. At some point he's shipping out. And whatever they have him doing, it's going to be dangerous. I don't want him distracted by me. If he doesn't come home, it'll be three lives shattered."

Tears sprang to Peggy's eyes as she pleaded, "I don't want you to have to read that telegram. If you tell me to walk away, I will. I will. I love him that much."

Seeing Peggy's anguish as she pledged to walk away forever if asked, Doris was gripped by a powerful instinct to embrace and comfort the distressed young woman. This girl seemed to truly love her son, despite having nothing to gain except responsibility and hardship.

But try as she might, Doris could not bring herself to reach out. Her heart still railed against the idea of losing Robert to this unexpected new family. Offering compassion felt like acceptance of her stolen future.

Doris sat paralyzed, tears shining in her own eyes. She knew Peggy meant no harm, that life had simply dealt them all an uncertain hand. But for now, comforting this heartbroken stranger still felt a sacrifice too great for a mother's love.

THAT'S HOW IT GOES

Chapter 5

SUMMONED TO DUTY

GRACE DRURY GATHERED UP her textbooks and notes after another grueling day of nursing instruction. Her head still spun from memorizing anatomical diagrams and medical procedures. She was more than ready to escape the stuffy classroom for some fresh air.

Just as she reached the doorway, her instructor called her back. "Miss Drury, can you return, please?" she requested. "These officers would like to speak with you."

Turning back, Miss Drury saw that a senior nurse leader and Army colonel had entered the room. She pivoted quickly, standing in firm attention.

With a mix of curiosity and unease, Miss Drury studied the officers' somber expressions. She racked her brain trying to think if she had made any missteps in training that would warrant an unexpected visit. Steeling herself, she resolved to take whatever criticism might come with chin held high. She was proud of her dedication, if not her natural nursing talents.

"I'm Lieutenant Colonel Stevenson. This is Captain Hiltz. Do you have a moment?" the senior officer asked.

"Yes, of course," Miss Drury replied.

"We've been tasked with putting together the Army Air Forces first medical air evacuation unit. It'll be composed of surgeons, medics, anesthesiologists, and of course, nurses. We'll be focused primarily on evacuating our wounded from the Pacific theater, given the remoteness of some of the islands," Lt. Colonel Stevenson explained.

Accustomed to lectures on anatomy and procedures, she sensed this impromptu meeting was leading somewhere unexpected.

"You've been evaluated as the top nurse in this class. Physically fit, smart, natural leadership skills, calm under pressure. You're a good nurse," Captain Hiltz praised while glancing at her clipboard.

"We need good nurses. This will be a difficult assignment. You'll be flying in and out of dangerous hot spots, under enemy fire. You're going to be treating the worst of the wounded and seeing a lot of death. Nursing at 10,000 feet in choppy weather while dodging flak is nothing like being at a hospital," the captain warned soberly.

The gravity of the war's human toll weighed heavily on Miss Drury as she envisioned young men like Robert Hickman and Sal Variano facing mortal combat. The captain's words about testing her fortitude rang true. She pictured terrified young men crying out for mothers they might never see again, their blood staining her hands.

"We think you have what it takes to be in our initial class of air evac nurses, and we would like you to consider this assignment. Are you married?" Lt. Colonel Stevenson asked.

"No," Miss Drury replied simply.

"Are you attached? Do you have a fiancé or boyfriend?" Captain Hiltz inquired.

Miss Drury paused slightly, looking confused. "No," she stated again.

"Good. That makes you the ideal candidate," Captain Hiltz remarked approvingly.

"Take a day or two to think it over. This isn't a decision to make lightly. This is purely a voluntary assignment," Lt. Colonel Stevenson advised.

"Count me in," Miss Drury stated without hesitation.

"What?!" Lt. Colonel Stevenson and Captain Hiltz exclaimed simultaneously, clearly stunned.

"You've asked me to consider. I've considered. When do we start?" Miss Drury asked resolutely.

"Immediately. You'll be shipping out to Hawaii in two days for additional training," Lt. Colonel Stevenson informed her.

Lt. Colonel Stevenson and Captain Hiltz exchanged pleased but astonished looks. With her swift agreement, they had just recruited the first nurse for the Army Air Forces' groundbreaking new Medical Evacuation Unit.

Though the risky assignment would surely push her fortitude beyond anything she had faced before, Miss Drury did not hesitate to volunteer. This was her chance to directly save lives on the front lines, and she would seize that opportunity without flinching.

***

The bustling hum of City Hall receded into the background as Robert Hickman took Peggy's arm, and together they walked toward the front of the hall. His uniform felt uniquely heavy and constricting today.

After haltingly proposing to Peggy just yesterday, Robert realized he didn't have a clear plan for their sudden nuptials. Yet somehow, here they stood, ready to take the plunge hand in hand.

Robert stole a sideways glance at Peggy as they neared the Justice of the Peace already waiting expectantly. Her simple floral dress and demure hat could not conceal the radiant glow brought on by impending motherhood.

Catching Robert's eye, Peggy gave his arm a gentle, reassuring squeeze. Despite the unconventional circumstances, in this moment her faith in their future shone through.

Robert surveyed the nearly empty hall. The lone witness sat slumped in a chair looking thoroughly bored by the proceedings. Just then, the creak of the heavy wooden doors made Robert turn.

Striding purposefully down the aisle was none other than his mother, Doris, an astonishing sight given her outrage the night prior. Yet now she clutched a bouquet of flowers, determination etched on her face.

Coming to a stop beside Peggy, Doris gave Robert's stunned bride a sad half-smile. Then taking her place at Peggy's side, Doris nodded to the Justice of the Peace, signaling the ceremony should commence.

As the officiant began solemnly leading them through their vows, Robert stood dumbfounded by his mother's dramatic change of heart. Doris met Robert's gaze, love and resignation mingling in her moist eyes.

With his stalwart mother embracing Peggy into the family, Robert's voice rang out clear and true as he pledged his eternal devotion. Surrounded by the two staunchest women in his world, he felt invincible.

After sealing their union with a heartfelt kiss, Robert embraced his new wife and then his courageous mother. Whatever challenges lay ahead, they would face them together as Hickman women always had—with quiet strength passing gently between generations like the bouquet of flowers.

***

The lights again dimmed in movie houses across America as audiences settled in for the latest weekly newsreel update. Gripping firsthand glimpses of faraway battlefronts had become vital information sources amid the unease of war.

"The first major land offensive in the Pacific theater took place at a little volcanic strip called Guadalcanal, the largest of the Solomon Islands," the narrator's dramatic voice boomed. "The United States Marines heroically captured the strategic airfield, and after months of bloody fighting, Allied Forces turned back the Japanese invaders for good."

On the screen, blurry footage showed Marines raising the Stars and Stripes above the captured Henderson airfield as cheering comrades looked on.

"From this stronghold at Henderson Field, the Allies will have a new perch to go on the offensive!" the narrator declared triumphantly. Stirred murmurs rippled through the darkened theater.

The scene shifted to show tanks rolling through a dusty North African landscape. "In the European theater of operations, Major General Dwight Eisenhower orchestrated the successful amphibious assault of French North Africa, the most complex invasion ever of its kind, delivering a punch in the nose to Hitler's so-called impregnable Third Reich."

Footage revealed throngs of Moroccan civilians jubilantly waving and tossing flowers at American tanks rumbling through the streets of Casablanca. "After only days of fighting, General George S. Patton's 39,000 American forces captured the strategic port of Casablanca and he was greeted as a conquering hero by the people of Morocco."

Seated in the jeep leading the procession was the familiar rugged face of Sal's older brother, Tony Variano, cigarette dangling rebelliously from his mouth. Having heard of Tony's daring exploits via hacked radio signals, the audiences swelled with pride at his prominent role in liberating North Africa.

As the screen dimmed, spirits were buoyed by these first tangible signs of Allies regaining strategic footholds. The newsreels brought the war's shifting tides home in dramatic fashion, cementing American resolve.

***

Tony Variano entered the Allied headquarters tent and crisply saluted the awaiting officer. Though weary from weeks of hard fighting, Tony stood tall. He had earned the respect of his fellow soldiers through brave leadership under fire.

"What's your first name, Private?" the unfamiliar officer inquired.

"Anthony. I go by Tony," Tony supplied promptly.

"You're now Corporal Variano," the officer informed him. "The men trust you, Variano. They respond to you. Where is your family from?"

"Italy, sir," Tony replied.

"I figured that, Variano. I mean where in Italy?" the officer pressed.

"A place called Anzio, sir. A fishing port south of Rome," Tony specified.

"You speak *Italiano*?" the officer asked.

"*Si Signore, parlo molto, bene*," Tony confirmed in fluent Italian.

"That's good to know, Corporal," the officer replied approvingly. "You fight with a chip on your shoulder, Variano, like it's personal. I like that. Keep up the good work, Corporal."

Tony saluted the officer sharply. Turning crisply, he exited the tent with his head held high.

A look of immense satisfaction spread across Tony's face as he walked away. The officer's words resonated deeply, recognizing the vengeance that fueled Tony's determination against Mussolini's fascist forces.

Having faced distrust for his heritage before Pearl Harbor, Tony felt compelled to prove Italian-Americans' loyalty on the battlefield. Now with North Africa liberated, he swelled with pride at playing an integral role in dealing Mussolini's empire a mighty blow.

Tony had earned this promotion through tireless courage under fire. He would continue leading his men bravely, spurred on by the quest to prove his worth and see justice done.

***

Izzy Variano fidgeted in the crowded pew, impatient for Mass to conclude. But as Father Nardechia solemnly took the pulpit, the sadness weighing upon the parishioners signaled this would be no routine Sunday service.

"Let us take a moment as we honor and remember the brave souls from our community who have lost their lives to this terrible conflict," the priest began heavily. "Let us offer our prayers and extend our support to the grieving families who bear the weight of their tragic absence. Lord, hear our prayers as we remember Private James Jonathan Vondrak ... Sergeant Michael P. Doyle ... Private Nicholas Anthony Romano ..."

Izzy watched her parents bow their heads mournfully as Father Nardechia read the names of local boys who would never again sit beside their families in this sanctuary.

Her heart nearly stopped when the priest uttered, "And Lieutenant Michael Sean Creighton."

Gasps echoed through the church at the name of their beloved teacher who had quietly enlisted after Pearl Harbor. Izzy grasped her father's sleeve, scarcely comprehending the devastating news. Leaning in close, she whispered urgently into her father's ear, "Mr. Creighton—our teacher from school!" Her words only deepened the anguish on her father's face.

"May they find peace in the arms of our Lord," Father Nardechia prayed. "Let us pray for an end to this darkness that plagues our world."

"Amen," the congregation whispered brokenly.

Afterwards, an oppressive silence hung in the church. Izzy sensed that her mother's glistening tears and father's stony expression belied their inner anguish. She thought of her brothers far from home facing untold dangers, and suddenly the sunny June morning felt very cold.

Looking around at the tear-streaked faces of families clinging to shreds of hope for their boys overseas, Izzy finally comprehended war's horrific toll. These were not just names uttered at Mass, but cherished sons and brothers they might never embrace again.

On this heartrending Sunday, Izzy left behind the last remnants of childhood. From now on, she would clutch her family closer and cherish each ordinary moment as the rare gift it was. Izzy now understood life's fragility in the face of evil sweeping the globe and taking Norwalk's finest far too soon.

***

The dense Texas humidity hung languidly as the rumble of heavy bombers permeated the Randolph Field complex. Crews scurried purposefully across the tarmac, guiding lumbering Flying Fortresses toward runways amid the orchestrated chaos. Nearby, a handful of impassive Air Forces brass surveyed the action, clutching notebooks and surveying the scene through dark aviator glasses.

In the soaring control tower, a radar operator stared intently at the screen, clutching the radio microphone as he calmly spoke. "Flying Eagle, you are losing altitude. Report status immediately."

He scrutinized the blinking dot representing Flying Eagle as it drifted downward. Moments passed without response as the distant growl of straining engines grew louder.

"Flying Eagle, this is Tower," the operator repeated evenly. "You are losing altitude. Please report status."

Only crackling static replied as a smoking B-17 emerged into view, its left engine trailing thick plumes. The bomber wobbled unsteadily, limping back toward the airfield.

The operator maintained his composure, though his knuckles whitened imperceptibly on the microphone. Whatever crisis was unfolding in the cockpit above, his duty was to guide the stricken aircraft home safely.

Tommy Murphy gripped the yoke tightly. The engines roared deafeningly around him. His plane was losing altitude fast, and his instruments were going haywire. Beside him, his co-pilot had gone ghostly pale, paralyzed by uncertainty.

A loud bang suddenly reverberated through the cockpit as the plane violently rattled. Warning lights began illuminating everywhere as Tommy desperately tried adjusting the throttle. But he could feel they were still dropping at an alarming pace.

"Tower, we just lost our number three and four engines!" Tommy yelled into his radio over the din. "I'm trying to adjust the throttle, but we're losing altitude fast."

"Flying Eagle, maintain heading two-seven-zero," the operator's crackling voice replied. "Try restarting the engine."

Tommy frantically tried to restart the dead engine, but it was unresponsive. "It's not responding. I can't get it back" he reported tersely.

The co-pilot's panicked voice rang out, "We're at 7,000 feet and descending!"

Though his own heart hammered wildly, Tommy forced himself to stay calm. With half their power gone, he had to somehow glide this wounded bird safely back to Randolph Field. Failure meant certain death for all on board.

Tommy pushed everything else from his mind, focusing only on keeping them airborne. He could taste fear in his mouth but swallowed hard. With the field looming in the distance, he wasn't giving up yet.

"Feathering the left propeller and increasing power to the right engine," Tommy reported, working quickly to try stabilizing the doomed aircraft.

"Roger that," the radio operator replied. "Descent is not slowing, Flying Eagle."

The plane continued its rapid descent, trailing smoke from the dead left engine. Tommy pushed the right engine harder. "Increasing more power to the right engine," he yelled over the din. "Trying to maintain heading two-seven-zero."

The voice over the radio informed him, "You're drifting, Flying Eagle."

Tommy made adjustments desperately, calling back, "Compensating for the drift. Right aileron and rudder. Stabilizing drift."

Just then the plane rattled violently again, nearly jolting Tommy from his seat. "Increased turbulence!" he shouted into the radio. "Descending rapidly!"

The panic rose in the co-pilot's voice as he screamed, "Murph, we're at 4,000 feet and dropping!"

There was no choice left, Tommy realized grimly. "Tower, losing altitude fast," he reported tersely. "Looks like the cowling is peeled back, creating extra drag. We're not going to make it back to Randolph Field. Looking for a spot to put her down."

Peering out the window with one eye while wrestling the controls with both sweaty hands, Tommy scoured the rural terrain below for an emergency landing spot.

"Flying Eagle, maintain two-seven-zero and come back to Randolph!" the radio operator urged desperately.

"Negative, Tower. We're rolling too hard," Tommy shouted back. "Proceeding with emergency landing."

Through the cockpit glass Tommy spotted a clearing bordered by farmland not too far away. With no other options left, he aimed the smoking aircraft toward the field. Sweat poured down his brow, but Tommy's eyes remained steely and focused.

The ashen co-pilot sat motionless beside him, numb with shock. But Tommy had to stay sharp for both their sakes.

"Tower, found a clearing to the west," he reported tersely. "Flaps set to full. Preparing for emergency landing. Maintaining approach speed, altitude decreasing."

"Hold her steady, Flying Eagle," the radio operator coached. "Descending too quickly. Emergency crew en route to farm west of Randolph."

The airfield was a speck in the distance now. There was no turning back. "Altitude decreasing," Tommy confirmed, lining up for the final approach over the wheat field. "Final approach. Bracing for impact."

The plane slammed down hard, skidding wildly as its belly absorbed the brunt of impact. The right wheel snapped off and the crippled aircraft lurched violently sideways, tilting up onto one wing. For a heart-stopping moment, Tommy was sure they would fully roll and erupt into a fiery inferno.

By some miracle, the mangled bomber groaned to a stop just shy of flipping completely over. It left a trail of hissing, smoldering destruction gouged into the earth, but somehow held together intact.

Tommy sat frozen, scarcely believing they had survived the harrowing ordeal. As the adrenaline rush subsided, overwhelming relief washed over him. Against all odds he had managed to bring them down safely.

Sirens pierced the heavy Texas air as emergency vehicles raced away from the Randolph Field complex across the tarmac. Their urgent wail shattered the ominous quiet that had momentarily fallen over the base after Flying Eagle's mayday call.

As the ambulances sped toward the wheat field trailing plumes of dust, a handful of impassive Air Forces brass emerged hastily from their building. Clipboards and notebooks lay forgotten back inside as they scrambled to board staff cars and join the rescue efforts.

An hour later, still trembling from the emergency landing, Tommy clutched a mug of coffee in the briefing room, trying to gather himself. His flight suit was plastered with sweat that had soaked through during the white-knuckled minutes aloft. Though exhausted, he knew that more questions awaited about his handling of the situation.

Three commanders entered briskly, their medals glinting under the harsh fluorescents. Tommy swiftly stood at attention before being directed to sit back down.

"Remain seated, cadet. That was some impressive work up there today," began the senior officer approvingly. "We've read the full tower report and spoke with your co-pilot. The kid could barely squeeze out a word, but what little he said was: 'Thank God for Murph.' It's Thomas, right?"

Tommy nodded silently, depleted of words himself.

"Can I call you Murph?" the commander asked. Tommy nodded again.

"That was a gutsy call up there, Murph," he continued. "Tower said they wanted you to try for Randolph Field. What made you decide to bail for the farm?"

Summoning his last reserves of energy, Tommy recounted his fateful decision. "We were too low, too hot, with too much drag. I could see the cowling had peeled back on the dead engine. I knew I could make it to the farm, and I knew I could get her down safely, sir."

One of the other commanders asked excitedly, "Took a lot of nerve, kid. We don't see a lot of cadets overruling the tower. Some people get ruffled by that sort of thing. You know what I call it?"

Tommy shook his head uncertainly.

"Leadership," proclaimed the commander.

"I call it stones," one commander declared. "Takes a lot of stones. Especially with your co-pilot on the fritz."

The senior officer nodded gravely. "Yeah, that's a whole other story," he agreed. "Anyway, just wanted to say we're proud of you, Murph. This is dangerous stuff. We've already lost three cadets this month. And we'll surely lose more. It doesn't get any easier in Europe."

Tommy's mouth went dry at the mention of more cadets perishing. The commanders' words underscored the ever-present specter of death looming over them all.

"The Royal Air Force tells us that twenty percent of their crews don't make it back each bombing run," the senior officer continued heavily. "That's a life expectancy of five runs. We're requiring crews to fly twenty-five missions. We're going to need smart, tough pilots like you who can hold it together under fire."

The officers rose to exit, but the senior commander added, "Stay seated, Murph. Take a few days off. We're proud of you, son."

After they departed, Tommy remained slumped in the hard metal chair, utterly depleted. Though praised for his composure under pressure, inside he still trembled from his narrow escape. The commander's grave words about the deadly odds facing them in Europe chilled Tommy to the core.

Could he summon that same steely courage time and again when lives hung in the balance? Would he beat the grim statistics facing pilots in combat? Despite his moment of glory, doubt and dread clouded Tommy's thoughts about the lethal missions looming ahead.

***

The frozen air stung Sal's cheeks as he stood alone on the snow-dusted sidewalk. Shouldering his duffel bag, he approached the idling bus that would start his journey home. Other uniformed men jostled past him eagerly, ready to return to the loved ones awaiting their arrival.

Taking a deep breath, Sal hoisted himself up the bus stairs. He made his way down the crowded aisle, exchanging nods and tight smiles with the other occupants. Finding an empty bench halfway down, he settled in by the window as the bus rumbled out into the night.

Sal watched the lights of camp fade into the distance with mixed emotions swirling inside him. He was ready for a respite from the grueling routine of training but reluctant to confront the worry he knew awaited back home. His lighthearted letters had glossed over the rigors and dangers of preparing for war. Returning to that anxiety-filled household weighed heavily on Sal's heart.

The next morning, Sal wandered slowly through the bustling department store in Times Square where Robert had first met Peggy. Soft holiday music filled the air as Sal searched the crowded aisles for gifts to brighten his sisters' spirits, if only for a moment.

Picking out modest presents, Sal hoped these small tokens might bring some cheer to a home darkened by dread. Exiting into the softly falling snow, his arms laden with packages, Sal tilted his face skyward. The peaceful flakes kissed his cheeks, lifting his mood slightly.

Boarding the train back to Connecticut that evening, Sal found an empty row and settled in by the window once more. He placed the neatly wrapped packages on the seat beside him and propped up his feet with a tired sigh. Exhaustion swiftly overtook him as the train rocked gently onward through the winter night.

Sal was jolted awake by the conductor calling "Last stop, Norwalk!" Gathering his gifts and bag, he stepped out into the chill night air once more, this time onto a familiar platform. Glancing around, Sal saw his parents had not come to fetch him. Likely they were busy with final Christmas Eve preparations at home, he reasoned.

Trudging the familiar route by foot, Sal soon found himself approaching the cozy Variano homestead. He hesitated just a moment on the front steps, bracing himself. Sal pushed open the front door and was immediately engulfed by his thrilled young sisters rushing to embrace him.

Beaming brightly despite the dark circles under her eyes, Carmela bustled over to pinch Sal's cheeks and envelope him in a crushing hug. Over her shoulder, Sal glimpsed his father, Giuseppe, hovering in the doorway, a tired but grateful smile creasing his weary face at the sight of his son safely home once more.

Later, sitting across from his father at the dining room table, Sal felt his stomach rumble as Carmela began setting out dish after delicious dish. The savory scents transported him right back to childhood, when his mother's home cooking offered comfort amidst boyhood trials.

"Ragazzi, beni qui mangare," Giuseppe called out. "Chiudete la radio."

At his command, Sal's sisters switched off the radio playing "All or Nothing at All" by Frank Sinatra and came to take their seats. An expectant hush fell over the room as Giuseppe bowed his head to say grace.

"Benedici, o Signore, per questo cibo che stiamo per mangiare," he intoned solemnly. Sal and his sisters reverently made the sign of the cross before eagerly digging into the feast.

As he ate, Sal tried engaging his uncharacteristically quiet sisters. "How do you like your presents?" he asked. "Have you had a chance to use them yet?"

The girls exchanged uncertain looks, seeming confused by his gift choices. "I haven't taken the pieces out yet," Izzy finally replied. "I'm hoping it comes with instructions. I don't think they move like checkers pieces."

Eager to bridge the divide, Sal offered, "Sure, I can teach you chess later. We play it on the base all the time. It really helps pass the time."

He left unsaid how the games also offered a brief respite from the gnawing loneliness and anxiety that hung over the trainees. Simply making it through each day felt triumph enough, with thoughts of the future pressed from weary minds.

Izzy quickly changed the subject, eyeing her brother eagerly. "What's it like flying a plane?" she asked. "Scary? I bet it's scary."

"Well, I'm not actually flying the plane," Sal explained. "I'm learning to be a navigator. I help with directions to make sure we reach our destination."

"Like with maps?" his younger sister Maria piped up.

"Yes, we have maps and other instruments," Sal elaborated, puffing his chest out slightly with pride. "Sometimes we even navigate by the stars."

He looked at his parents meaningfully. "The crew relies on me to get them to and from our target," Sal impressed upon them. "It's a lot of responsibility." "*Molta responsabilita*," he added in Italian.

His parents nodded approvingly, warmed by their son's sense of duty.

"We saw Tony on the newsreel the last time we went to the movies," Maria suddenly recalled. "They showed him somewhere ..." She turned to Izzy for help placing their older brother.

"Northern Africa," Izzy supplied. "He was riding in a Jeep."

Sal looked genuinely surprised to hear of Tony's starring role, but knowing his headstrong eldest brother's quest to prove Italian-Americans' loyalty, Sal just chuckled and remarked, "Doesn't surprise me. Tony has it in for that Mussolini."

The more his sisters peppered him with wide-eyed questions, the taller Sal stood. If he could ease their worries by portraying navigator training as a safe, proud role, fudging the harsh realities seemed a small sin. Inside, Sal still trembled at the unknown dangers ahead. For now, though, he would paint the bright picture they needed.

The sisters seemed more interested in questioning Sal than touching the feast before them.

"Are you going to see Tony or Joe when you're in the war?" Maria asked eagerly.

"Well ... um, I don't know," Sal faltered, caught off guard. "I'm not sure whe—"

But Maria barreled on, "When do you go?"

"I don't know. We're still in advanced trai—" Sal tried explaining before she cut him off again.

"Will you go to Europe like Tony or the Pacific like Joe?" Maria pressed.

Overwhelmed by the rapid-fire inquisition, Sal grasped for answers. "I really don't know," he confessed. "They don't tell us where we're headed, we find out whe—"

Maria immediately interjected, "Where do you want to go?"

Sal was at a total loss by now. "I guess I haven't given it much thou—" he began before Izzy seized the baton of interrogation.

"Do you have a girlfriend?" she asked curiously. "Are you getting married? I hear all the soldiers are getting married before they ship out. When are you getting married?"

Sal was completely flustered by the rapid-fire questions. His mind raced furiously, grasping for an evasive answer.

Izzy continued her pleading, saving Sal from a response. "Can you take us to the movies?" she asked hopefully. "We haven't seen 'Holiday Inn' yet. All my friends say it's darling. Bing Crosby isn't Frankie, but I like that song, 'White Christmas.'"

Relieved at the change of subject, Sal quipped lightly, "Well, as soon as you two stop talkin' and start eatin'. *Mangiare! Mangiare!*"

The girls finally turned their attention to their neglected plates. Just then, the doorbell rang, interrupting the moment.

Rising from the table, Sal went to answer it. When he reentered the dining room a few moments later, his face was ghostly pale. Shoulders slumped, he stood frozen in place, a clutched telegram dangling from his limp hand.

"Chi era quello?" Giuseppe asked in confusion. But Sal did not respond, staring vacantly ahead.

"Ho detto, chi era quello?" Giuseppe repeated more insistently.

Visibly trembling, Sal struggled to find his voice. "It was Western Union," he finally uttered weakly. "I have a telegram."

Hands trembling violently, Sal read the devastating words that would haunt him forever:

"The Navy Department deeply regrets to inform you that your son, Seaman First Class Joseph Angelo Variano, went missing in action and is presumed deceased in the performance of his duty and in the service of his country while on board the USS Juneau during the battle of Guadalcanal. To prevent possible aid to our enemies, do not divulge the name of his ship or station. If further details are received, you will be informed. Please accept our heartfelt sympathies. Rear Admiral Randall Jacobs, Chief of Naval Personnel."

Though his parents grasped little English, their shattered expressions left no doubt they understood the horrific message. Carmela covered her mouth to stifle a cry, then bolted from the room in anguish. Giuseppe sat gripped in silent torment, head cradled in his hands.

Sal's young sisters began sobbing uncontrollably, their stouthearted brother having met a violent end alone at sea. The telegram slipped from Sal's limp fingers as he stood paralyzed in place. He could feel himself retreating deep within, going numb to dull the searing pain.

This couldn't be real, his heart screamed in denial. Just this morning, his family had been whole and hopeful. Now their world lay torn asunder, future happiness ripped away without warning by war's savage toll.

The cheerful bustle of Christmas Eve preparations had vanished, replaced by inconsolable weeping mingling with the radio's crooning carols in mockery of their devastation. The jarring juxtaposition made Sal want to retch as he stood frozen, praying to wake from this agonizing nightmare.

The anguished sobs that filled the room offered crushing proof that no awakening awaited. Death had intruded on their holiday, leaving Sal to pick up the pieces of his shattered family.

THAT'S HOW IT GOES

Chapter 6

SHATTERED HOLIDAYS

ON CHRISTMAS EVE, military barracks took on a festive spirit as homesick young recruits sought to make cold bunks feel celebratory. The 20-year-olds had adorned the dreary plywood walls with an odd mashup of holiday decor and risqué pinup girls.

The lively notes of "When Johnny Comes Marching Home" by Glenn Miller suddenly crackled from the phonograph, lifting spirits around the barracks. The smooth backing harmonies of Tex, Marion and the Modernaires filled the bunks with a bittersweet nostalgia. Some recruits immediately sprang to their feet, pulling each other into enthusiastic swing dances to pass the lonely holiday eve.

Others huddled in clusters, their faces flickering in the string lights as they lost themselves in animated conversation and holiday nostalgia. A few lone souls were scattered about the periphery, busying themselves with shooting dice or tapping their feet to the music.

Seated on a bottom bunk in the corner, Robert scratched intently with his treasured Empire State Building pen, pouring his swirling thoughts onto paper. Gripping the red pen like a lifeline, he wrote furiously, filling page after page in his neat script.

The lively phonograph tunes and exuberant voices seemed to fade into the background as Robert crafted each line just for his beloved Peggy. He knew these letters offered her vital reassurance amidst gnawing worry back home.

> I'm counting the days till I have leave, and I can visit you, Mom and the baby. I love the pictures, please do send more. She definitely has your button nose and bright eyes. The guys pass a lot of pictures around, but usually Betty Grable or Rita Hayworth. Of course, not me! Me and Harry Shapiro are the only ones showing off baby pictures! Some of the boys are homesick, I guess I am too. But I try not to think about it. They're keeping us busy all right. I'm usually too tired to feel anything. The guys are beginning to get anxious about what's next. We still don't know when we'll be shipping out, or where. A few of the guys brag about winning the war by themselves, but I think they're just hiding their

fear. It's easy to talk tough in front of the guys, lots of us do that.

But it's harder when you're alone with your thoughts. I'm not sure where I fit in it all. I keep to myself mostly, try to focus on our training. I have only one close friend, a guy named Jimmy Sefton, from White Plains. I think about Sal and Murph a lot. I hope they're managing okay. Knowing you, Mom and baby Margaret are doing well is about all I really need. Counting the days till I see you again.

Love, Your Robert.

After covering several pages front and back with his neat script, Robert finally set down his pen. He had poured his swirling blend of holiday nostalgia, gentle optimism, and homesick yearning into this latest letter. Carefully folding the precious pages, he tucked them into his shirt pocket for safekeeping.

Glancing up from his corner perch, Robert realized he was so absorbed in writing that he hadn't noticed the lively Glenn Miller song fade out. In its place now blared a rousing military marching tune, its energetic beat pulling more recruits to their feet in impromptu revelry.

Watching them link arms and circle the barracks in goofy camaraderie, Robert felt a pang of loneliness creep in. Writing letters allowed him to feel connected to his faraway mother and young wife, but once the pages were sealed and sent, the gnawing isolation of military life returned.

Caught up in melancholy reflections, Robert didn't notice the grinning recruit approaching until he felt a vigorous clap on his shoulder.

"C'mon, Hick, join in the fun!" the exuberant soldier implored, linking his arm through Robert's and pulling him to his feet.

Unsure, Robert glanced around at the ring of grinning faces circling past, beckoning him to shed his gloom and join their makeshift parade. Their youthful energy and carefree swaying stirred memories of childhood games long forgotten.

Despite himself, Robert felt an impish smile creep across his face. Giving his bunkmate's arm an answering squeeze, he allowed himself to be drawn into the infectious revelry. He had poured his heart out in ink; now was the time for fellowship.

Laughing, Robert fell into pace with the snaking line of recruits dancing goofily around the cramped quarters. For tonight at least, camaraderie would keep loneliness and doubt at bay.

***

Standing in the bustling movie theater lobby, Doris couldn't help but feel transported to simpler times. The aroma of buttery popcorn perfuming the air, colorful posters lining the walls, and Bing Crosby crooning "White Christmas" over the radio speaker ushered her back to weekends long past.

"I can't recall the last time I saw a movie. Before Robert left for bootcamp, I think. Seems like ages," Doris remarked wistfully to Peggy as they inched along in the endless concession line.

"It is nice to be out of the house, the first time I've been away from the baby," Peggy replied, though she looked slightly uneasy to be away from little Maggie.

Just then, Doris noticed a familiar slender youth in uniform chatting with two younger girls near the ticket counter.

"That looks like Robert's friend Salvatore, over there," Doris said, pointing across the crowded lobby.

Peggy followed her gaze to take in the soldier's appearance. Though she had never met Sal, Robert had described his mischievous army buddy in fond detail.

"He's one of Robert's friends. They enlisted together," Doris informed her. "The young man in the uniform, with his sisters, I believe."

Peggy studied the soldier and two fresh-faced girls curiously. Though homesickness and worry lurked beneath the surface, an afternoon at the pictures offered a pleasant distraction from the troubles awaiting them outside.

"Ah, yes. Robert's told me about Sal in his letters, that he's always singing," Peggy recalled fondly. "I think he's training to be a pilot or something. He looks too young to be in the army!"

Doris waved eagerly across the lobby, trying to catch the young soldier's eye. After a few attempts, he noticed her gesture and came over. His two companions stayed back by the ticket counter.

"Salvatore, so good to see you!" Doris exclaimed warmly as he approached.

"Hello, ma'am, a pleasure to see you as well," Sal replied politely, removing his hat.

"This is Peggy, Robert's wife!" Doris introduced him.

Peggy smiled and extended her hand. "A pleasure to finally meet you, Sal," she said. "Robert has told me so much about you!"

To Peggy's surprise, Sal revealed, "We've actually met before. Well, we didn't speak to each other, but I was with Robert that day in Times Square at your store."

Peggy's eyes widened in disbelief. "Really?" she replied. "I didn't know that he—"

"I could see you two were hitting it off—it only took him half the day to pick out a gift for you," Sal interjected, nodding towards Doris. With a knowing grin, he added, "So I figured I would leave you two alone. It seems to have worked out."

Sal chuckled in response.

A broad smile washed over Peggy as she realized Robert's Army friend had witnessed the genesis of their romance.

"It certainly has," Peggy affirmed, beaming. "I've actually moved in with Doris—I mean, Mom. She's helping with our daughter, Maggie."

"Except not right now—my sister has a shift," Doris chimed in with an amused chuckle. Her smile fading, she asked sincerely, "How have you been, Salvatore? We saw your brother Tony on the newsreel. He looked so dashing, so heroic. Your parents must be so proud."

Sal hesitated, clearing his throat awkwardly. "My parents are really hurting. So am I," he finally answered heavily. After a weighty pause, he continued, "Two days ago we found out that my brother Joe was missing in action. His boat was torpedoed near Guadalcanal."

Sal's voice took on a brittle edge. "They've been to Mass four times already, praying for him. They're hoping for a miracle. Sometimes sailors survive." He seemed to be trying to convince himself as much as them. "He might be okay. That's what I'm telling myself. Maybe somewhere he's okay."

A stunned silence followed, the cheerful lobby chatter fading into the background. Tears shining in her eyes, Peggy gently grasped Sal's elbow, hoping the simple touch might offer some small measure of comfort in his profound grief.

"I've told my sisters that the Navy will find him, that he'll be okay," Sal shared somberly. "I don't know if they believe me or not. I don't know if I believe me. But I'm trying to be hopeful."

He paused, adding quietly, "I thought maybe the movies could take our mind off things, at least for a little while, before I head back to the base. I—I just—I hope they can—"

His voice cracked with emotion and he couldn't go on. Doris looked back helplessly, at a loss for words. "Salvatore, I don't know what to say," she finally offered, her voice heavy with sorrow.

"We're both so very sorry," Doris said supportively. Grasping his arm, she added earnestly, "We will hold him in our prayers too. Please let your parents know we're praying for him and if there's anything I can—we can do—please let us know."

"I will. Thank you," Sal replied, clearly moved. "It was a pleasure seeing you again, Peggy," he added before heading back to rejoin his sisters.

Doris and Peggy were left staring at each other, hollowed out by sadness and dread. A chill ran through them as they imagined Robert facing similar, deadly perils overseas. They had tried to armor themselves against the ever-present specter of tragedy, but stark anguish still managed to pierce through.

Seeing the Variano family's optimistic holiday torn asunder was a forceful reminder that no loving home was immune to war's savage whims. As they pondered Sal's heartbreaking news, Doris and Peggy silently vowed to cherish every moment fate allowed them. For in times like these, nothing was guaranteed except tomorrow's uncertainty.

***

The pilot's urgent warning cry of "Hold tight, folks, incoming Zeros!" barely registered in Nurse Drury's ears over the C-47's monstrous droning engines. This was her first air evacuation run ferrying wounded from the hellish battle raging below on Guadalcanal.

The transport plane violently shuddered as bursts of flak exploded perilously closely outside. The deafening roar swallowed all attempts at communication. Gripping her seat for dear life, Nurse Drury's wide eyes took in the plane's sparse interior converted into a rudimentary flying hospital.

One of the physicians gestured urgently to secure any medical equipment not yet tied down before it went crashing through the shuddering fuselage. Working quickly alongside two other nurses, they made sure everything was as stable as possible while the C-47 bucked like an enraged bronco.

Peering out a small window, Nurse Drury glimpsed terrifying sights of the fiery battles raging beyond the plane's thin metal skin. Below, Guadalcanal smoldered under relentless Japanese assault.

Zeros swarmed angrily around the transport like wasps, raining machine gun fire against its flanks. Just then, a group of intrepid Marines in their F4U Corsair fighters swooped in boldly to intercept the Zeros. An intense midair dogfight erupted as Nurse Drury watched helplessly through the window.

THAT'S HOW IT GOES

Chapter 7

BAPTISM BY FIRE

TRACERS STREAKED PAST in a dizzying pattern as the embattled aircraft performed lethal acrobatics. Nurse Drury held her breath, willing the American planes to prevail.

Nerve-wracking minutes seemed to stretch into eternity. Then the tide turned in the dogfight raging around their plane. The skilled Corsair pilots finally gained the upper hand; one Zero after another was sent flaming toward the sea, plunging and spinning with plumes of smoke trailing behind them.

As the triumphant American fighters broke away, one even dared an absurdly close flyby right past the C-47's cockpit. Nurse Drury glimpsed the name "Boyington" emblazoned below its canopy as its pilot nodded to their own. She offered up a silent prayer of thanks for these fearless pilots risking all to protect the vulnerable flying hospital and its precious human cargo.

With the swarming Zeros vanquished, an eerie calm settled over the transport plane as it descended toward Henderson Field. The violent shuddering and flak bursts ceased, though the engines maintained their deafening drone.

The C-47 transport shuddered as it touched down on the crude runway gouged into Henderson Field's volcanic rock. Even before the plane fully stopped, the side doors were sliding open and Marines swarmed aboard carrying gravely wounded comrades.

Nurse Drury found herself in the center of the grim chaos as the evac crew swiftly loaded over two dozen bloodied young men inside. Working alongside the doctors, she helped assess injuries and make the men as comfortable as possible atop the bare metal benches bolted to the plane's stark interior.

In the blur of activity, one battered Marine caught Nurse Drury's eye. He looked no older than 20, his ashen face glistening with sweat. Crimson soaked through the hastily applied bandages swaddling his abdomen.

As the young man was eased down, he let out an agonized groan that knifed into Nurse Drury's heart. She knelt swiftly beside him, brushing damp hair back from his clammy forehead. His half-open eyes were glassy with pain and confusion.

All around them, the roar of the C-47's engines filled the cabin as the flying hospital raced back into the clear blue skies. The punishing noise made medical chatter difficult and the doctors continued assessing injuries as best they could. Nurse Drury tuned out the relentless drone, focused only on the pained young man before her.

"What's your name, Marine?" Nurse Drury asked gently, taking his limp hand in hers.

"Raymond ..." the young man mumbled almost inaudibly. "Ray Lauria." He grimaced, fresh beads of sweat rolling down his battered face.

"Where am I?" he whispered weakly.

"We're at 10,000 feet headed towards Hawaii," Nurse Drury explained, keeping her voice calm and soothing. "We're gonna patch you up and get you home. I need you to stay with me. Can you do that?"

But the Marine just groaned softly, seeming not to register her words. His eyelids fluttered as he hovered at the edge of consciousness.

Nurse Drury gave his hand an urgent squeeze. "Can you do that?" she implored, her voice edged with rising fear. "I need you to stay with me. Who is waiting for you back home? Who is gonna give you a big hug when you get back?"

She searched his face intently for any flicker of response, and prayed that her words would somehow anchor him to life.

"Mom," the wounded Marine suddenly mumbled nearly imperceptibly, his eyes still closed.

He shivered violently, fresh sweat beading on his waxy skin. "I'm cold," he whimpered through chattering teeth.

"Okay, let's hold on for Mom," Nurse Drury urged, blinking back tears. "She can't wait to see you."

Gently smoothing his damp brow, she pleaded, "Let's hang on for Mom. Okay?"

The Marine's breathing grew more ragged as he hovered at death's door. Then in a barely audible whisper he pleaded, "Sing to me."

Nurse Drury recoiled slightly, not sure she had heard right. "You want me to sing?" she asked.

"Sing to me," the delirious young man repeated weakly, "like when I was a kid." He let out another low moan that seared through Nurse Drury's chest.

"Sing to me, Mom," the Marine pleaded once more, his voice barely a whisper.

Nurse Drury's heart shattered. This brave young man would never make it home to hear his real mother's song again.

Unsure what else to do, she haltingly began singing the first gentle lullaby that came to mind. Her untrained voice cracked with emotion and the tender words flowed from her soul.

"That's how it goes, when you're in need of someone ... who understands the way you feel," she crooned softly.

As she sang, Nurse Drury suddenly recognized the song from that day at the recruitment center, when Robert and Sal had enlisted so eagerly. The memory nearly choked her voice away.

Clasping the Marine's hand tightly, she watched helplessly as he slipped away. A single tear traced down her cheek. With her other hand, she gently caressed his ashen face.

Around them, the din of the plane and blur of medical activity continued unabated. Nurse Drury blocked it all out, focused only on providing this dying boy some measure of comfort in his final moments.

She had trained tirelessly, yet no training could have prepared her for the anguish of this intimate loss. Nurse Drury refused to succumb to despair. Instead, she silently vowed to fulfill her duty with even greater courage and compassion from this day onward, buoyed by the hopes of those like this stranger who had sacrificed everything.

***

The merciless Georgia sun beat down on the airborne jump school complex. Inside a makeshift fuselage of a C-47 plane, Robert waited tensely alongside eleven other trainees in full gear. Their jump instructor paced like a caged tiger, barking orders and critiquing every move.

"Ready! Jump!" the instructor yelled, as the first trainee hurled himself from the four-foot platform into the dirt below. The men landed hard, tucked into practiced rolls, then swiftly scurried clear. A sign on the mock plane read, "Never Repeat the Same Mistake!"

"C'mon!" the instructor shouted at the winded recruits. "Next! Keep moving! A skilled jumper is an alive jumper!"

As the last man completed the drill, the instructor added sharply, "You hate me now, but you'll thank me when it's for real!"

The next exercise was atop a menacing 200-foot jump tower. Robert watched as the trainee before him stepped to the edge.

"Drop your paper!" the jump master ordered through his megaphone. The jumper released a slip of paper to gauge wind speed and direction.

"Three, two, one, *drop*!" the instructor bellowed. The man dropped rapidly, legs flailing wildly as his bungee harness snapped taut just above the ground.

"Keep those feet together!" the instructor roared through his megaphone. "I said feet together, jumper!" Turning to the chagrined trainee, he shouted, "You just broke an ankle, jumper!"

As the man rejoined the line, the instructor added, "A safe jumper is a jumper with his bones intact!"

Steeling himself, Robert stepped forward. Feet tightly together, he prepared to prove his readiness by leaping bravely into the void.

Over the grueling weeks of jump training, Robert had slowly transformed from a nervous novice into a seasoned professional. Under the withering scrutiny of the instructors, he had mastered every skill through sheer determination.

Now in a vast parachute hangar, Robert labored intently on the silken canopy spread before him. Every fold had to be perfect. A single mistake meant almost certain death. Half a dozen instructors, faces carved from granite, silently patrolled the space like prison guards.

Nearby, one of the instructors suddenly grabbed another jumper's half-packed chute in disgust. "Jumper, you just splatted!" he barked, shoving the botched bundle back into the flustered young man's arms. "Start over! A second chance at life!"

Robert's pulse quickened, but he forced himself to focus. He had to get this right. Another instructor stopped behind a different trainee, reaching into his pack. "Sloppy, jumper, sloppy!" the instructor scolded. "I see broken bones in your future!"

Robert's hands trembled slightly, but he carefully made each crease with precision. Just then, the head instructor announced sternly, "This isn't a game, jumpers! Take this seriously!" After a pause, he added "If you can't hack it, you can always go back to being a leg!"

At the insult, the recruits responded as one, "AIRBORNE!" Robert intoned the word with all his spirit, fueling his determination. He would not wash out. Checking his work, he saw no mistakes. He had mastered this life-saving skill under immense pressure. Robert allowed himself a flicker of pride at having shown his grit.

After proving themselves under punishing pressure, the recruits now faced their potentially toughest test yet: holding their tongues through an entire silent meal under the instructors' eagle-eyed supervision.

Seated amidst more than six dozen fellow trainees in the mess hall, Robert mechanically shoveled in bites of the bland chow without tasting it. The cavernous room rang with an unearthly silence, broken only by the clink of utensils against plates.

The instructors had ordered absolute quiet during meals to drill self-discipline into the unruly young men. Just one sound could bring group punishment raining down.

A deafening clatter rang out suddenly when one hapless recruit's fork hit then bounced on the floor. Robert froze, not even breathing as the chaotic noise echoed.

Moving as one, the seventy-five recruits then leapt to their feet and roared, "AIRBORNE!" at the top of their lungs in solidarity. The outpouring of camaraderie drowned out all else for a glorious moment.

Whatever punishment awaited, they would face it together. Grueling days had forged them into brothers. *Let the instructors do their worst*, Robert thought fiercely. Together, the young men of Airborne were quickly becoming unbreakable.

***

As the Saturday matinee crowds settled into their seats, an air of anticipation filled the darkened theater.

The screens flickered to life and audiences leaned forward intently. "The Allied forces in the Pacific begin 1943 with a hard-fought victory at Papua New Guinea, reclaiming the island from the Japanese invaders," proclaimed the narrator's stirring voice.

Gripping footage showed American forces raising the flag above Papua New Guinea's strategic airfields as the enemy's strongholds smoldered in the distance.

"It's a major setback for Imperial Japan, halting their expansion southward towards Australia and isolating their outpost at Rabaul," the narrator declared. "Military brass say the strategic airfields will provide a base of operations for reconnaissance and supply missions across the Pacific region."

An approving murmur rippled through the crowd at news of this decisive momentum shift.

The scene shifted to show President Roosevelt and British Prime Minister Churchill conferring intensely around a table. "President Franklin D. Roosevelt and British Prime Minister Winston Churchill met for ten days in the liberated city of Casablanca, following the Allies' successful campaign in North Africa, to plot strategy for the eventual invasion of continental Europe."

The narrator concluded dramatically, "Both men agreed that the only acceptable outcome to the war was 'unconditional surrender' by the three Axis Powers, Germany, Italy and Japan. The two leaders made it clear that their intent was not to punish the people of the Axis countries, but rather to restore to them their sacred right of democracy."

As the screens faded to black, resolute applause broke out. With the Allies regaining their footing, victory was starting to feel tangibly within reach.

Chapter 8

OVERSEAS

HANDS SHOVED CASUALLY into his pockets, Tommy gazed up at the soaring gray hull of the waiting troop transport ship. All around him jostled fellow bomber pilots, trading jokes to mask their nerves as boarding time neared. A large banner hanging from the ship's side boasted "Liverpool or Bust" in bold lettering.

"Well, Murph, ready to show these Brits how we do things stateside?" called out a grinning pilot, clapping Tommy supportively on the back. Tommy smiled weakly in return, the ever-present knot in his stomach tightening. He kept up a confident facade, yet doubts plagued his thoughts about the deadly bombing raids ahead.

As they filed up the gangplank, hundreds of hooting GIs already crammed aboard the ship's deck greeted the new arrivals rowdily. Watching the leaden Atlantic surf churn below, Tommy felt untethered, unsure if he'd ever again stand on familiar American soil. There was no turning back now. Come what may, the die was cast. This transport carried him inexorably onward into the great unknown.

That evening in the cramped, raucous mess hall deep within another transport ship's bowels, Sal perched on a table improvising soulful tunes to a captive crowd of appreciative GIs. Strumming his guitar, a crewmate provided backup as Sal crooned smoothly into an imaginary microphone.

The impromptu concert momentarily drowned out the ever-present rumble of engines and lap of waves against the hull. Transfixed faces revealed that Sal's golden voice conjured cherished memories of loved ones awaiting their safe return.

Launching into a soaring final note, Sal basked in the enthusiastic cheers and applause, but that bravado masked inner unease about the deadly serious duties ahead. For now, he would gift his fellow servicemen a few hours' relief from dreadful thoughts of combat through the healing power of song.

Days later, Sal found himself on Pearl Harbor's docks about to board a bus. He slung his duffel bag higher on his shoulder and took in the tranquil tropical scene. Palm trees swayed gently under clear blue skies as seabirds wheeled overhead. The salt breeze carried no hint of the destruction dealt here such a short time ago.

Tommy stepped off the gangplank onto the chilly docks at Liverpool, instantly missing the warmth of the Texas sun. All around him, fellow American bomber pilots pushed forward as they disembarked, eager to set foot on dry land after the long journey across the Atlantic.

Tommy fell into animated conversation with two pilots, using dramatic hand gestures as he enthusiastically recounted the dice games they'd played to pass the time aboard the transport ship. Gambling had helped keep their minds off the harrowing missions awaiting them in Europe.

Glancing around the dreary port, Tommy noted the lines of idling buses ready to take them to the Royal Air Force base where they would receive final training. The bland landscape and gray skies felt alien compared to home, but he knew that warm receptions likely awaited them inland from British civilians grateful for America's support.

As he walked toward the waiting buses, Tommy felt mixed emotions churning inside. The excitement of experiencing a foreign place contrasted with pangs for the familiarity of home. Yet, he thought, adventure called and there was no turning back now. Wherever the winding road ahead might lead, he would face it with his brothers in arms at his side.

***

Peggy sat cradling baby Maggie on the well-used but comfortable couch in the Hickmans' cozy living room.

The infant was finally drifting off to sleep after an afternoon of fussing.

Just then, the front door burst open and Doris breezed in, crackling with unusual energy. Tossing her coat and hat hastily onto the rack, she made a beeline for the couch.

"Hi, Mom, you have a good day at work?" Peggy inquired, mildly surprised by Doris's buoyant demeanor.

"I did!" Doris replied brightly as she settled onto the couch. *There's an odd zip in her body language,* Peggy observed, wondering what lay behind the older woman's high spirits.

"It sure seems like it. Did you get a letter from Robert at work?" Peggy guessed hopefully. Her son's vivid letters often lifted Doris's mood.

Doris had even bigger news. "I resigned!" she announced proudly. "Actually, I took what they call a leave from the accounting firm. Mr. Morgan told all the clerks that we could take a leave if we wanted to go work at the textile plant near the high school."

Peggy's eyes widened in surprise. Doris had worked at that staid accounting firm since she was practically a girl. What could have inspired the sudden departure?

Doris could see the questions forming on Peggy's face. Leaning in conspiratorially, she explained, "They need extra hands in the textile factory now that so many men have gone off to war. And I'll be making parachutes!"

Comprehension dawned on Peggy as Doris continued enthusiastically. "It's vital work for the soldiers. I'll be helping protect boys just like Robert when they make their jumps."

Peggy's eyes widened in surprise. "Wait, slow down. You did what?" she asked incredulously.

Doris could barely contain her enthusiasm. "The Army is temporarily converting the textile plant down the street for the war effort, to make tents, parachutes, field dressings, bags, that sort of stuff," she explained rapidly.

"They're short on manpower, so they're recruiting women to help. Mr. Morgan asked if any of us clerks wanted to work there, and I said yes! He said we'd have our clerk jobs back once the war is over."

Peggy sat stunned, trying to process this unexpected turn of events. "Wow," she finally managed. "If I didn't have my hands full I might do the same thing." She smiled down at the now-dozing baby in her arms.

"When do you start?" Peggy asked.

"Tomorrow!" Doris replied eagerly. "I can't wait to tell Robert in my next letter!"

Peggy carefully transferred the sleeping infant into Doris's arms as she talked. "I think he's going to be shocked but so proud of you for helping with the war effort," Peggy said supportively.

Doris gently rocked the baby, her expression softening. "I've been in that accounting job ever since his father passed," she mused. "Mr. Morgan has been very good to us. But something told me to say yes when he asked." A smile lit up her face and she added, "Two other women from the office will be joining me. They both have boys overseas too."

Peggy studied Doris's glowing expression, sensing the deeper emotions behind this abrupt career shift. Inspecting the parachutes that might someday save soldiers like Robert gave Doris a way to protect all the faraway sons.

Though initially stunned, Peggy now felt immense admiration for Doris's selfless act. They would both do whatever it took to bring their loved ones home safely, even if it meant stepping bravely into the unknown.

***

The days at the Army hospital in Honolulu blurred together for Nurse Drury as she tirelessly cared for the grievously wounded soldiers evacuated from Pacific battlefronts. Each young man under her care was someone's beloved son, brother or husband; she resolved to offer them comfort and companionship along with expert medical treatment.

Some afternoons found her seated at the bedside of a heavily bandaged soldier, patiently reading aloud letters from his sweetheart back home. Though the soldier could not speak through the gauze enwrapping his face, his one visible eye watched her intently and he drew strength from the familiar words.

Other times, she stood holding the hand of a young man encased in casts and in traction, whose cheek she gently caressed as he endured the long, painful road to recovery. Her compassionate touch reminded him that he was more than just a broken body in need of mending.

When spirits needed lifting, Nurse Drury engaged in cheerful banter with the soldiers as they ate, giving them a sense of normalcy amidst the chart notes and needles. Laughter momentarily made the sterility of the ward feel homier.

Invariably, the cruel realities of war also intruded. One morning, another nurse entered the recently vacated room where Nurse Drury lingered. Her somber expression instantly conveyed the tragic news that its occupant had not survived the night. Though such losses never grew easier, Nurse Drury steeled herself to provide care and solace to the next battered soul.

Come what may each day, she resolved to be a healing presence offering compassion, companionship and resilience—vital medicines for the heart and spirit.

Exhaustion weighed heavily on Nurse Drury as she sat outside the Honolulu Army hospital, seeking a brief respite from the nonstop intensity within its walls. Beside her on the bench sat the senior nurse officer who had recruited her for the pioneering air evacuation team.

The officer studied Nurse Drury's drained expression with concern. "Air evac is every bit as grueling as we thought it would be when we formed this unit," she remarked somberly. "It's just the harsh reality of war. We're surrounded by death. We do the best we can, but no matter how many lives we save, there are some that aren't going to make it."

She paused, letting her words sink in before adding gently, "I wish it weren't the case, but that's the awful truth."

Nurse Drury kept her gaze fixed on her feet, acknowledging the statement with a faint, "I know ... I know." The ceaseless tide of shattered bodies and lives was taking an immense emotional toll for which her training had not prepared her.

The senior officer leaned in, trying to catch Nurse Drury's downcast eyes. "This isn't easy stuff," she said understandingly.

Nurse Drury remained staring at the ground, retreating deep within herself. She could not articulate the anguish of losing patients—often mere boys—day after day, who were ripped violently from life. Outwardly she maintained her professional composure, but inside her spirit was buckling under the weight of so much suffering.

For now, she needed this moment of silence to gather strength for the next wave of broken souls needing her care.

The senior officer studied Nurse Drury with concern. "You've seen more suffering in two months than anyone should see in ten lifetimes," she said heavily. "I wish I could tell you that it'll get easier, but it won't."

Nurse Drury finally lifted her gaze. "If it means making myself numb to seeing these boys die—shutting down my feelings—then I don't want it to get easier," she stated resolutely. "I'd rather suffer inside than stop caring. I'll live with whatever toll that takes on me. They deserve that."

The officer looked back, visibly moved by Nurse Drury's profound empathy yet uncertain how to respond.

After a thoughtful pause, she said carefully, "I understand, I really do, but we need you for the duration of the war. Not many nurses can deal with the pressure of air evac. That's why you're here."

Her tone became urgent as she continued, "All I'm asking is for you to pace yourself. We don't know when this damn war will be over. If you let yourself get torn up with every run, you won't make it. I've seen it happen. You'll end up breaking."

Nurse Drury met the officer's concerned gaze unflinchingly. After a long, weighted pause, she stated, "I'll take that chance."

With that, the two women sat in pensive silence. Nurse Drury again lowered her eyes to stare distantly at the ground, steeling herself for the anguished duty ahead. She would not harden her heart nor retreat from the grief, no matter the personal cost. Her compassion made her invaluable in this brutal conflict that spared no one from loss.

Though the officer's warning rang true, Nurse Drury refused to spare herself if it meant also sparing these soldiers the depth of care they deserved. She would bear witness to their sacrifice, honoring it with an open heart.

THAT'S HOW IT GOES

Chapter 9

THE HOMELAND

PREDAWN STILLNESS HUNG OVER the waters off Sicily's southern coast as Tony Variano's landing craft cut through the misty gloom. All that could be heard was the steady roar of engines and the rhythmic crash of waves against metal hulls. Tony stood poised at the front of the bobbing vessel, salt spray nipping his face.

Consulting the map of Sicily one last time, Tony used crisp hand signals to issue final instructions to the thirty men crammed behind him. The liberation of the imprisoned island hinged on this audacious Allied assault catching the enemy off guard.

Peering through binoculars, Tony scanned the rapidly approaching shoreline. Rocky cliffs loomed out of the fog, but there were also stretches of beach that would have to serve as the Allied foothold. Gela's strategic port could then be captured and allow reinforcements to flood in.

A sudden crash of waves nearly jolted Tony from his feet but he barely flinched, focused solely on the objective ahead. Icy water soaked through his uniform but Tony stood steadfast, clutching his map. After today, the Sicilian people would taste freedom once more. He would see to it personally.

A thunderous blast of heavy artillery abruptly shattered the morning quiet. From the cliffs, bursts of German flak filled the sky as Tony's craft neared the beach. Heart hammering, Tony braced himself for the fight of his life that would release the homeland he loved.

***

Robert waited impatiently in the noisy barracks hallway, receiver pressed to his ear. His buddy Shapiro had just finished a marathon call home, finally relinquishing the hall's lone telephone.

At long last, Robert heard his mother's voice answer. "Hi, Mom," he said, relief washing over him. "Yes, it's really me. Shapiro hogged the phone for an hour. I finally wrestled it away. How are my girls?"

Miles away in Connecticut, Doris cradled the phone on her shoulder, gently rocking baby Maggie in her arms. On the couch nearby, Peggy was passed out from exhaustion.

"We're doing just fine," Doris replied warmly. "Peggy is napping, poor girl is exhausted. I'm trying to rock the baby to sleep."

Though disappointed that he couldn't hear his bride's voice, Robert smiled, picturing the cozy scene. "Sounds perfect," he said wistfully. "Wish I was home to take it all in."

Doris hesitated before asking delicately, "Will we see you before you ship out?"

Robert frowned. "I don't know," he admitted. "Our training is intensifying. I doubt we'll get any more leave. I really don't know though."

He could sense his mother's worry through the phone line's crackle. "Whatever you're doing must be important," Doris remarked carefully. "I hope it's not too dangerous. All the girls at work, their sons and husbands are overseas already."

"And how is work? How does it feel to be part of the war effort? Have they made you a colonel yet?" Robert chuckled lightheartedly.

Doris smiled at his gentle teasing. "Just doing my part," she replied. "Someone once told me we all have to do our part." She laughed along with her son.

"I really like it," Doris continued earnestly. "Every day we're making things for the boys overseas. We all feel good about it. I miss my old friends, but I've made new ones. On Thursday nights we stay late, bring some dishes we've made, eat dinner and catch up. Everyone is anxious for updates from their loved ones."

Robert's smile faded slightly, knowing the worry his own role caused. "Well, I'm sure our troops appreciate it. I know I do," he said sincerely. "This hasn't been easy on anyone. I have to run."

He hesitated before adding gently, "Give Peggy and Maggie a kiss for me."

"Love you," Doris replied affectionately.

"Love you too," Robert answered softly.

"Write when you can," Doris continued, trying to spend a few precious extra seconds with her son."

"Yes, I'll write you soon. Promise," Robert assured her. "Bye."

After exchanging loving farewells, Robert reluctantly hung up. The line of impatient guys waiting their turn still stretched down the hall. A few made exaggerated smooching sounds, ribbing Robert good-naturedly about his call home.

But Robert just grinned, refusing to let their teasing get to him. The ribbing was a small price to pay for a few priceless minutes of connection with his family. Their love armored him for whatever lay ahead.

Stepping aside, Robert waved the next eager soldier over to make his own call. As he made his way back to the noisy barracks, Robert kept replaying his mother's voice in his mind. No matter the distance between them, he drew strength knowing she was out there under the same stars, keeping the home fires burning.

**

Tommy Murphy stood at attention alongside fellow pilots and crew inside the bustling operations building. Their eyes were glued to the curtained map at the front of the room as they awaited today's briefing.

The rumble of an approaching Jeep outside heralded the arrival of Colonel Keith Merrill, commander of the

306th Bomb Group. Tommy watched as the colonel briskly entered, trailed by several subordinates.

Reaching the front, Colonel Merrill ordered, "At ease, men." The room of tense young soldiers sat down in unison, eager to learn their target for today's mission.

With a flourish, the colonel pulled open the curtains to reveal the giant map of Europe. Tommy leaned forward intently, searching for telltale strings marking their destination.

"Today's target is Emden," the colonel announced, eliciting quiet murmurs as he pointed at the map of Germany. "We'll be heading for the factories and oil refineries on the south end of town. We can expect heavy fighter and anti-aircraft resistance. The weather is overcast. We can expect little change in overall conditions. The ceiling will be under ten thousand feet."

He let this dire news sink in before continuing solemnly. "Our secondary target will be the naval facility and U-boat pen to the east at Wilhelmshaven. It's a key base for German operations in the North Sea."

The colonel tapped the map location and emphasized gravely, "We will hit the secondary target whether or not we hit the primary target. In other words, gentlemen, today there will be two targets. Is that understood?"

Seeing heads nod, the colonel moved on briskly. "The flares of the day for fighter support will be red, green, green to the target, red, green, red coming off the target. Any questions?"

Hearing none, he concluded crisply, "All right, let's do some damage today, gentlemen. Dismissed."

As the crews noisily exited, the colonel called out, "Murphy, hang on a second."

Tommy halted, pulse quickening. Turning back slowly, he approached the colonel, wondering what dire news awaited.

He stood at attention, bracing himself as Colonel Merrill began solemnly. "You're going to be lead plane today. We're going to face a lot of resistance up there. The Jerries know we're coming for the U-boat pen. They'll be waiting for us."

The colonel's tone was deadly serious. "We'll need everyone in tight formation. We have to have maximum impact over both targets. There's no margin for error on this one. The brass are counting on us to prove that precision daylight bombing works."

Tommy swallowed hard, the enormity of this responsibility hitting him. As lead plane, the entire squadron's success depended on his piloting and nerves holding steady amidst the lethal flak. One lapse in concentration could doom them all.

But Tommy simply gave a broad smile and snapped a crisp salute, concealing his swirling unease. "I won't let you down, sir," he declared confidently.

The colonel returned the salute, his steely gaze conveying the operation's gravity. Tommy strode briskly from the room, maintaining his aura of assurance. Inside, his stomach churned with dread about spearheading this decisive and likely suicidal raid into the heart of enemy airspace.

Once outside, Tommy's confident expression finally cracked. Finding a secluded corner, he leaned against the wall and closed his eyes, trying to slow his hammering heart. This was the chance he had trained for, to prove his mettle at the war's fiery crucible. Now that the moment had come, Tommy could scarcely breathe for fear of the hellish flames ahead.

Hours later, Tommy guided his battered B-17 down the runway, the weight of duty finally lifting from his shoulders. As the ground crew directed them to a stop, Tommy let out a shaky breath, scarcely believing they had survived.

The mission had tested Tommy to his limits, both physically and mentally. Navigating through dense cloud cover, he had relied on instruments alone to maintain a tight formation lest they collide midair. Bursts of flak constantly threatened to blast them from the gloom, but he'd held firm.

Approaching the primary target, Tommy had steeled his nerves and aligned for the bombing run. Anti-aircraft fire erupted all around, peppering the wings and fuselage. But Tommy stayed the course, releasing his payload directly on target.

After hitting their secondary objective despite relentless pounding, Tommy had nursed the battered bomber home through worsening weather. Now safely on the ground, overwhelming relief washed over him.

Clambering down last from the plane dubbed "Lucky Charm," Tommy felt anything but lucky. Though he kept up a triumphant facade, inside he trembled from the grueling ordeal. But the mission was complete, and Tommy had proven his grit under devastating enemy fire.

Shortly thereafter, Tommy stood uneasily in Colonel Merrill's office, still on edge after surviving another harrowing raid. As the colonel and Major Ryder discussed the mission, Tommy tried tuning out their chillingly casual debrief.

"Major, what was the final tally?" Colonel Merrill asked, pouring himself a drink.

"Eighteen of twenty-one returned, sir," Major Ryder reported. "Nash's plane bailed over the channel. Air-Sea Rescue fished them out. They're banged up, but nobody's missing."

Tommy released a breath he hadn't realized he was holding. Nowadays, every crew that made it back felt like a minor miracle.

"Good. How many do you think can go tomorrow?" Colonel Merrill continued briskly.

Major Ryder grimaced. "Max twenty. We're short on parts. The crew will be working all night to get us to that. Some of these birds are being held together with spit and glue."

The colonel took this in stride. "All right, push them to get to twenty. Everyone that can go, goes." Turning to Tommy he offhandedly asked, "Murph, can I get you a drink?"

Tommy mutely shook his head, wanting nothing more than to escape the colonel's nonchalant debriefing. The day's trauma still clung to him, while the brass seemed utterly detached from the hellish realities high above.

Settling on the edge of his desk with drink in hand, Colonel Merrill callously concluded, "It won't be a milk run tomorrow, gentlemen."

Tommy looked back incredulously. Milk run or not, he knew death always flew alongside.

"Major, bring the strike photos as soon as they're ready," Colonel Merrill directed. "I'm hoping the pictures confirm what the boys are saying. Got our orders from the old man. We're going back tomorrow to finish off our secondary."

Tommy's chest tightened, but he spoke up resolutely. "They'll be waiting for us again, sir. That's the heaviest fighter coverage we've seen yet. And the flak was thicker than storm clouds."

But the colonel waved off Tommy's concerns. "The word is out, Murph. Daylight bombing is working. The losses are heavy, but the damage is real. The old man says German production is slowing."

After a weighty pause, he dropped the next bombshell. "You're leading again tomorrow, Horowitz takes high group; Rollo takes low."

Before Tommy could react, a German announcer's voice suddenly crackled over the radio. Colonel Merrill hastily turned up the volume.

"This is Germany calling, Lord Haw Haw talking from Berlin," the sinister voice informed. "We send special greetings today to the misguided American pilots from the pilots of the Luftwaffe."

The announcer continued tauntingly, "Your so-called friends in the Royal Air Force have duped you into these daylight missions because they are too cowardly to try it themselves. How do we say that you're guinea pigs? The Luftwaffe will eagerly be greeting you again tomorrow, especially the Three hundred and Sixth out of Ashbury.

Our top ace, Friedrich Steiger, can't wait to add to his tally of forty-four kills. He has his eye on you, Lucky Charm. Tomorrow, you won't be so lucky."

Colonel Merrill quickly snapped off the radio, but the damage was done. Tommy stood frozen, pulse hammering. The Germans somehow knew their bomber's nickname and were lying in wait once more. He would be leading the sheep to slaughter, if he even survived another trip over the target.

Colonel Merrill tried waving off the dire propaganda broadcast. "Ignore Lord Haw Haw. Just Jerry propaganda. They're getting nervous. We're getting through," he insisted.

But Tommy wouldn't be placated so easily. "With all due respect, sir, he didn't call you out!" Tommy retorted urgently. "Steiger dusted Hardy and Zimmerman today, Fitzy two days ago. He's been feasting on us."

The colonel's expression hardened. "Tighter formations, Murph," he directed sternly. "Hold the group integrity. We need maximum coverage. Don't think up there. Just react. They'll follow your lead."

Tommy hesitated, then gave a solemn nod. "As a friend back home likes to say, whatever key you're playing in, I'll sing along to it," he acknowledged resolutely.

Colonel Merrill clasped Tommy's shoulder and walked him to the door. Though racked by doubts, Tommy maintained a stoic front. He knew the colonel was right—he had to be the rock holding his men together no matter what lethal chaos swirled around them.

Stepping outside, Tommy took a deep breath of night air to still his nerves. Though his hands still trembled, tomorrow he would grip the controls unwaveringly, leading his men onward through hell itself. Their fate would rest in his steady hands.

***

The scorching South Pacific sun beat down on Sal as he joined his crew boarding their B-24 Liberator, dubbed "Coral Grable" after pinup girl Betty Grable. Sal felt a rush of pride as he gazed at the colorful nose art of bombshell Betty in a tropical setting.

Climbing inside, Sal kissed his hand and patted the fuselage twice for luck, as was his ritual before each mission. Though still a superstitious gesture, touching the bomber's metal flank stirred fond memories of his high school hobby of singing to imaginary crowds. How far he had come from those carefree days.

Later, aloft amidst scattered clouds, Sal monitored his instruments as the drone of engines surrounded him. Miles of shimmering blue ocean stretched to the horizon below. Up ahead, the nearby Solomons were coming into view.

"How we looking, Sal?" called out pilot Frank "Cheech" Cavallo from the cockpit. "What's our ETA to target?"

Sal double-checked their course. "Looking great," he reported confidently over the radio. "Thirty seconds ahead of last checkpoint. Gives me time to take any requests from you guys. What'll it be?"

Groans resounded over the headsets at the prospect of another impromptu concert. "Anything but Sinatra," joked the co-pilot wearily. "Give us some Grable."

Sal shifted smoothly into a spot-on Clark Gable impression. "Frankly my dear, I don't give a damn," he declared dramatically over the radio.

"I said Grable, not Gable, you idiot!" the exasperated co-pilot shot back.

Grinning, Sal launched into a sultry Mae West impersonation. "Why don't you come up and see me sometime?" he purred suggestively.

The bombardier chimed in over the headset, "Someone get Caruso to the bomb bay. We can drop him on the enemy position. Maybe that'll get the Japs to surrender."

"Or harakiri," the co-pilot quipped.

Thoroughly enjoying himself now, Sal broke into a gravelly James Cagney voice. "Why you dirty little rats!" he exclaimed, eliciting more chuckles throughout the plane.

Dropping the impression, Sal added breezily, "Just wait till we're in Hawaii next month on leave. All them hula honeys are gonna be swooning to this golden voice. Maybe I'll cut youz in on the action if you're nice to me."

Though his antics irritated some, Sal knew his impressions and singing lifted spirits in the air. He would play the clown to keep doubts and dread at bay, if only for these precious moments above the clouds.

"We'll keep that in mind, Caruso," Cheech replied, a smile in his voice.

Just then, the radio operator broke in urgently. "Change in coordinates, Blue Eagle. Japanese convoy veering slightly."

"Understood. Standing by," Cheech responded.

Sal swiftly began recalculating their flight path. "Alright, signor Cheechio, need to adjust our heading fifteen degrees due west," he reported.

"Roger that. Co-pilot, prepare to make adjustment," Cheech directed.

"Adjusting heading to two-seven-five degrees," confirmed the co-pilot.

"Maintain course," instructed Cheech. "Sal, confirm next checkpoint. Let's stay on schedule. There's some Jap supply ships that have a date with the bottom of the ocean."

More chuckles sounded over the radio at their imminent deadly rendezvous. Cheech added soberly, "Keep an eye out for Zekes. It won't be smooth sailing forever."

"Roger that," replied the tailgunner, punctuating his words with a round fired skyward. "Throat all clear. We're ready."

Sal intently monitored his instruments as Cheech banked the lumbering bomber onto the new heading. Up ahead, the jungle-strewn Solomons loomed through scattered clouds. Though buoyed by camaraderie, Sal knew peril awaited somewhere in that tropical paradise; he would guide them through with steady hands, come what may.

***

The lights in the crowded theater dimmed as the newsreel footage shimmered to life. An excited hush fell over the audience, eager for the latest gripping dispatches.

"Italy's Zero Hour has arrived!" the narrator proclaimed dramatically. "The Allies' mighty air and sea armada hammered the Nazis and retreating Italians at Salerno, Calabria and Taranto, leaving the Italian government in chaos. Benito Mussolini, the sawdust Caesar, has been kicked out of power. His balcony empire collapses."

The crowd leaned forward intently as footage showed Mussolini being toppled.

"General Dwight Eisenhower announces that the Italian army has surrendered unconditionally," continued the narrator. "Hitler's Nazi forces launch a fierce counteroffensive to occupy Europe's 'soft underbelly'—they won't go without a fight!"

The mood shifted as the scene changed. "In the Pacific, Allied sea and land forces continue to advance through the strategic Solomon Islands, culminating with the Third Marine Division storming the beaches of Bougainville, the largest island in the Solomon archipelago."

A swell of applause went up at this decisive headway.

"It's only a matter of time before the Japs are pushed all the way back to their home islands," declared the narrator triumphantly. "Emperor Hirohito is probably regretting their sneak attack on unsuspecting Pearl Harbor!"

As the newsreel ended, an energized murmur rippled through the crowded theater. The war's momentum was clearly on the side of the Allies, bringing hopes of victory tantalizingly close.

THAT'S HOW IT GOES

Chapter 10

SHIFTING MOMENTUM

A REVERENT HUSH filled the empty church as the diminished Variano family knelt silently in prayer. Giuseppe and Carmela bowed their heads solemnly, while young Maria and Izzy fidgeted slightly but tried to remain still.

At the front of the church glowed four prayer candles, one for each Variano brother serving overseas. The family's hopeful vigil had become heartrending after the devastating news of beloved Joe's disappearance at sea.

Kneeling in her customary spot, Carmela struggled to surrender her anguish and trust in God's wisdom, but each passing day without word of Joe's fate became harder to bear. She longed desperately for a miracle yet steeled herself against hopes that could be cruelly crushed.

Beside his weary wife, Giuseppe uttered the familiar prayers by rote, his thoughts consumed by churning emotions which no litany of Hail Marys could soothe. Powerless to protect his sons, he placed their fates in divine hands while barely containing the tempest within.

The young sisters squirmed numbly, their childlike faith rattled by harsh realities for which no Sunday School lesson had prepared them. They stole puzzled glances at the candle representing their beloved Joe, struggling to understand how a loving God could allow such injustice.

Together, the family clung to these precious moments of spiritual refuge. But devastation had infected even this sanctuary, leaving the Varianos to wrestle with profound questions in the lonely void between loss and meaning. Their tightening circle of light glinted against gathering darkness, vulnerable yet resolute.

***

A thin dusting of snow crunched underfoot as Doris hurried into the bustling Paramount Parachute building. Inside, rows of women at long wooden tables busily sewed parachute panels by the pale winter light filtering through frosted windows.

Later that evening, Doris and seven exhausted coworkers gathered wearily around a scrumptious homemade dinner spread laid out on overturned crates. Too tired to even remove their work coverings, they eagerly dug into the feast as Tommy Dorsey's "I'm Getting Sentimental over You" played softly from a nearby radio.

"I'm afraid to look outside. Has anyone seen how bad the snow is?" Gail queried between bites.

Donna shook her head. "Enough to be annoying, but not enough for snow chains," she replied wearily.

"This meatloaf is fantastic—who made it?" Gail continued, savoring a mouthful.

"I did," Doris answered, smiling. "It's my son Robert's favorite dish. The secret is adding a little brown sugar. It keeps it moist, livens it up a little. An 'explosion of flavor,' as he likes to say." She chuckled affectionately.

"How is he? Have you heard from him since he shipped out?" one woman asked.

"He spoke with Peggy two days ago. Called from England. I forget exactly where," Doris replied. "He told her the weather was lousy and the food was even lousier." She chuckled, picturing Robert's exaggerated eye roll. "Peggy said he was in good spirits, anxious to get on with it, whatever it is." Doris hoped her light tone concealed her gnawing unease.

"My sister Rosalie's son just arrived in England, too," Donna chimed in. "He told her there's a real buildup going on. My husband, Mike, said they're going to invade France at some point."

A frazzled woman declared emotionally, "I just want it to be over already. I hate the sleepless nights, the not knowing. I think about Tommy and Mikey all the time. Yesterday my neighbor got the telegram ..." Her voice trailed off as tears filled her eyes. "I can't take it anymore."

Doris reached over and gently squeezed her shoulder. She knew that haunting feeling all too well.

"So did Carol Hardy on the night shift," Gail added heavily. "Poor girl. Her husband, Bill. She's not even twenty-five. My heart just aches."

The radio announcer's words pierced the solemn mood. "That was Tommy Dorsey. Yes, we're all getting sentimental over our boys."

A hush fell over the room. Doris picked at her food, appetite vanished. The swirling snow outside mirrored the storm of emotions churning within. She longed desperately for her beloved son's safe return.

**

Robert leaned intently over the sand table map amidst five fellow soldiers in the dim, rain-lashed tent. Their commanding officer, Lieutenant Bill Summers, finished lighting a cigarette and addressed the group solemnly.

"You can finally stop pestering me about what's going on," Lieutenant Summers began wryly.

"We're swimming the channel to France?" Sergeant Nickels joked. A few mild chuckles sounded.

Lieutenant Summers flashed a hint of a smile. "You will be leg," he retorted. "The rest of us will be dropping from the sky."

Taking a drag from his cigarette, he continued gravely, "It's simple: Hitler controls France. Time to take it back."

Robert and the others responded in hushed unison, "Airborne." The significance of this moment was not lost on them.

"We don't know exactly when, but likely late spring," the lieutenant informed them. "That gives us time to train, train and train some more. We know that we're gonna be the tip of the spear. We'll need to know this operation frontwards and backwards so that we can perform it in our sleep. Take it apart and put it together blindfolded. That stuff back in the states was kids play compared to what we'll be up against. This is for real."

He paused, meeting each man's gaze before commanding crisply, "Staff Sergeant."

Staff Sergeant Flaherty stepped forward, his expression dire. "Not a word of this leaves this tent," he warned sternly. "You don't walk out of here with a single note or stitch of paper. And you don't breathe a word of it. As far as the company goes, we're just drilling and training, like always. Is that understood?"

Robert and the other men nodded silently, the weight of secrecy clear.

"You have the next three hours to memorize every centimeter of terrain here and here," Flaherty directed, indicating points just inland from coastal France, "and every tree and shrub that goes with it.. We don't get any do-overs, gentlemen. We'll need to take out the heavy gun batteries here and here ..."

He pointed to map locations as the men leaned in intently. "And secure this road here to prevent their retreat. It's critical that we accomplish our task. Is that understood?"

More solemn nods answered him. Robert's pulse quickened as his eyes devoured every detail. Failure was not an option with so much at stake.

"Any questions?" Lieutenant Summers asked.

Robert spoke up. "Will we see this map and tables again before jump?"

"Not unless something changes. Or if we get better information," Lieutenant Summers replied.

Sergeant Flaherty added sternly, "I'll be quizzing you at twenty-three hundred hours. If you don't know it cold—and I do mean cold—then someone else will be leading your team." He paused before emphasizing sharply, "Is that understood?" The men nodded, the message clear. Any lapse in preparation would cost leadership roles and jeopardize the entire operation. There was zero margin for error. "Then get to work," Flaherty ordered. He and Lieutenant Summers ducked out, leaving the four soldiers alone to meticulously study the sand table and terrain map.

Robert leaned in, heart pounding. Every ridge, river bend and coastal contour had to be seared into his memory. He would take nothing for granted in preparing for this hallowed task.

The hours ahead would push Robert to his mental limits. But he welcomed the challenge, knowing that even one missed detail could spell disaster on D-Day. The Allied invasion's success rested in no small part on his readiness to lead his men unerringly onto enemy shores. He would not fail them when the moment came.

***

The furious thunder of battle engulfed Tony Variano as he sprinted toward the burning lead tank holding up their advancing column. Machine gun fire and explosions erupted all around, but he focused only on reaching the trapped driver.

"Sergeant, that tank is gonna explode!" yelled the frantic lieutenant. "Take someone and get that driver out!"

Tony didn't hesitate. "Not enough time!" he shouted back. "I'll do it myself!"

He dove to the ground and scrambled on his belly through blistering fire to reach the tank. Flames licked its metal hull as Tony climbed atop and manned the turret gun. He rained suppressing fire at the enemy sniper nest, shielding himself behind the inferno.

The blistering heat seared Tony's skin, but still he fired relentlessly in all directions. As return fire slowed, he pried open the hatch with one hand while continuing to shoot with the other.

"I have them under fire!" Tony shouted down through the smoke and flames. "Get out now!" He sprayed bullets wildly to cover the driver's escape.

Seconds later, dazed man emerged from the hatch. Tony leapt from the tank and was slammed down, hit by machine gun fire mid-air.

THAT'S HOW IT GOES

Chapter 11

NO RETREAT

IGNORING THE SEARING PAIN, Tony dragged himself behind the tank's smoldering hull.

"Keep your head down, Sarge," urged a soldier, rushing over. "Let's get you to safety. They got you pretty good."

Tony winced as the pain intensified. "Where did I get hit?" he asked through gritted teeth.

"In the shoulder, bleeding badly," the soldier assessed. "We need to get you patched up."

He lifted Tony and started moving him away from the raging firefight. "You're gonna get the purple heart for this, Sarge," the soldier predicted. "Probably a trip home, too."

Tony shook his head adamantly. "I don't want no medals, and I ain't goin' home."

Medics hurried over as the tank column pressed onward.

***

The low drone of engines surrounded Sal as he flew with his crew aboard a C-47 transport bound for Hawaii. After weeks of grueling missions, they were finally getting a coveted break. Sal had talked nonstop about his plans to romance local girls, fraying his companions' patience.

"Sal, if we hear one more word about how many hula honeys you're gonna land, I swear we're gonna drop you over Midway on the way back," threatened Cheech wearily.

"Make that Tarawa," the bombardier chimed in. "We'll go out of our way."

Sal put up his hands in mock surrender. "I won't say another word. Not another word," he pledged, miming locking his lips. "I'll just let my charm do the talking. And trust me, my charm can talk up a storm!"

The bombardier rolled his eyes. "Your charm may work on the locals, but these USO dances are mostly army nurses," he cautioned. "They're all hardened battle axes. They're not falling for your routine, Caruso."

Sal just grinned and leaned back casually. He relished the thought of flirting with pretty nurses who had likely never before encountered his smooth Italian charisma.

"We'll see about that," he retorted breezily. "I'll have those angels of mercy eating out of my hand before long. Just you wait."

Seeing his crewmates' dubious expressions, Sal switched tactics. "All right fellas, what do you say I liven things up with a tune?" he proposed brightly. "Bing Crosby? Frankie? Or some Andrews Sisters?"

Without waiting for a reply, Sal launched enthusiastically into "Don't Sit Under the Apple Tree." His golden voice soon filled the transport's cabin, transporting the weary men far from war's harsh realities.

Later at the bustling USO dance, the ballroom was filled with GIs, nurses and local girls swaying to a live band's rousing rendition of "In the Mood." Sal circled the packed dance floor, scouting for prospects, when a familiar face stopped him short.

"I can't believe it's really you, Noletti!" Sal exclaimed, grabbing his old friend in an enthusiastic hug. "I didn't think I'd ever see you after you washed out of flight school."

His clumsy classmate grimaced good-naturedly. "The brass thought I was more suited to be a grunt," Marty conceded wryly. "They're probably right. My feet are meant to be on the ground, not up there."

Sal chuckled, recalling Marty's infamous blunders aloft. "Yeah, you're the only tail gunner I know who shot out his own plane's tail!"

"Yeah, well, I got lead in my own tail too," Marty quipped. "Got shot in the ass during Tawara. At some point I'll be able to ditch this walking cane."

Giving Sal a playful shove, he joked, "Don't go grabbin' my ass, Sal, it's still tender."

Just then the bombardier sidled up and nodded towards Marty. "Who's your girlfriend, Caruso?" he teased.

"Ease up, dipshit," Sal shot back breezily. "A buddy from flight school, Marty Noletti."

Though the dance's romantic prospects hadn't panned out yet, Sal was buoyed by the unexpected reunion with his bumbling former classmate. The camaraderie offered a refreshing break from the war's ever-present dangers.

The bombardier glanced skeptically at Marty. "I don't see any wings," he remarked.

"I washed out," Marty admitted with a shrug. "Sal, you still singin'?"

"The only time he shuts up is when we're over the target," the bombardier interjected wryly before Sal could respond.

Sal grinned, unaffected. "Noletti and I were part of a trio back at school with another *paesano*," he explained.

"Let me guess, you called yourselves the three guineas," the bombardier jibed.

Marty laughed. "We didn't, but everyone else did!"

The bombardier waved his hand dismissively. "Well, your guinea charm isn't gonna work on these army nurses," he declared cockily. "Stick with the locals and leave the nurses to me."

But Sal just flashed a confident smile. "We'll see about that," he retorted breezily. "I think the band is playin' my tune."

Handing his drink to Marty, Sal sauntered toward the stage and had a quick word with the bandleader. Seconds later, the lively swing music shifted to a smooth jazz intro. Sal grabbed the mic and launched into "I Can't Get Started."

The dance floor paused, couples turning toward the stage. Under the spotlight, Sal crooned with effortless charm that soon drew dreamy smiles from nurses and locals alike, his golden voice working magic once more.

Nurse Drury entered the crowded USO hall with three fellow nurses, scanning the dance floor curiously. The lively big band music made her toe tap, stirring nostalgic memories of carefree evenings back home before the war.

When the tempo changed and a familiar voice rang out singing "I Can't Get Started," she turned in astonishment to see none other than Sal Variano crooning soulfully into the microphone on stage.

A delighted smile spread across her face as she watched Sal pour his heart into the lyrics. His silken voice transported the enthralled crowd, but Nurse Drury felt he was singing just for her in that moment.

"'Cause you're so supreme, lyrics I write of you," Sal sang feelingly. "I dream, dream day and night of you. And I scheme, just for the sight of you. Baby, what good does it do?"

Swaying dreamily to the romantic tune, Nurse Drury was momentarily lost in memories of their chance encounters back home. Sal's unexpected presence tonight felt like an answered prayer, offering light amidst war's shadow.

She gazed up dreamily as Sal crooned, savoring having his golden voice all to herself. But glancing around, she realized a mob of swooning women, both nurses and locals, had moved front and center.

Sal was playing to the crowd now, leaning in cheekily as the lyrics poured from his heart. But amidst the adoring fans, his eyes conveyed a flicker of confusion.

Feeling suddenly foolish, Nurse Drury slipped away toward the exit. The intimate moment had vanished, leaving her just another awestruck face in his doting throng.

As the final notes faded, Sal found himself surrounded by female admirers, their perfumed bodies pressed close. His buddy Marty elbowed through to congratulate him.

"Sal, that was amazing!" Marty raved, returning Sal's drink. "You've got your pick of the litter!"

But Sal seemed distracted, craning his neck toward the doors. "Yeah, yeah, they got the right key," he muttered absently, barely registering Marty's words.

Polite smiles concealed Sal's unease as he extricated himself from grasping hands and batting eyelashes. Weaving through the crowd, his eyes desperately scanned for Nurse Drury.

"What's the matter?" Marty asked, bemused. "Go pick one of those nurses, or maybe two, and strut out of this place!"

Sal just frowned absently. "Yeah, I should. I—I just ... I thought I saw someone."

"Huh?" Marty replied, now thoroughly confused.

"I thought I saw someone I knew from back home," Sal tried explaining awkwardly. "Someone I—I ... someone I know. This girl—woman, that I—I ... I could have sworn tha—"

Marty waved his hands, stopping Sal's rambling. "Are you imagining stuff?" he interjected. "Sal, you have this whole place eating out of your hand. Stop hallucinating, you idiot, and go partake in the spoils of war."

"Yeah, yeah, I am," Sal mumbled halfheartedly. "I mean I will. I will."

But his eyes still desperately scanned the crowd for any sign of Nurse Drury. Seeing his friend's uncharacteristic distraction, Marty just shook his head in bemusement.

"Well, don't wait too long, Romeo, or Juliet might vanish into the night," he cautioned lightly before wandering off.

Alone now, Sal stood frozen in indecision. Had he imagined Nurse Drury's presence tonight? Or had he foolishly lost his chance by playing the flirtatious showman? His fluttering heart urged him to search for her. But what if she was just a beautiful dream that vanished with dawn's light?

***

Tommy gripped the controls tightly as his B-17 shuddered under intense flak bursts. All around, the bomber formation was swarmed by enemy fighters, the deafening chaos intensifying as they neared the target.

"Arrowhead Leader to all pilots, tighten formation!" Tommy ordered over the radio. "Repeat, tighten formation!"

"Six bandits, wait, no, eight bandits, ten o'clock high and closing fast!" a panicked voice reported.

Tommy quickly responded, "Lansing, they're headed for high group. Close the gap. Don't let them in!"

He glimpsed bursts of gunfire as his crew tried fending off the fighters buzzing angrily around them like hornets. Then another pilot yelled, "Blue Wing Two to Arrowhead Leader, Blue Wing Four is hit! Blue Wing Four losing altitude!"

Tommy's gut seized as he watched the stricken bomber spin out of control, trailing plumes of black smoke. Flak bursts continued rocking the formation as it limped relentlessly onward over occupied France.

"You've been hit, Smithy. Bail! I order you to bail!" Tommy yelled into the radio, wiping sweat from his eyes. The stricken B-17 kept steadily losing altitude.

Tommy realized with horror that Smithy's crew was trapped inside the burning plane, unable to escape their fiery fate. He forced down the lump in his throat.

"Navigator, how far from IP?" Tommy asked tightly, regaining some composure.

"Eight minutes from last checkpoint," came the reply over the intercom. "12 to go."

Tommy pounded his fist furiously on the control panel. "It's a goddam turkey shoot up here," he cursed through gritted teeth.

"Blue Wing Two to Arrowhead Leader, B-seventeen hit, two o'clock!" another panicked report rang out.

"Anyone jumping?" Tommy demanded urgently. "Anyone jumping?"

The response offered some relief. "Can't tell ... yes, I see one, two, three, four chutes at least!"

But there was no time to breathe. "Three bandits, twelve o'clock high! They're right on top of you, Fossy!" a pilot screamed over the channel.

"Evasive maneuvers, Foss!" Tommy ordered. "Get him some help!"

The chaos was never-ending. Tommy tasted bile rising in his throat but forced it down. He had to guide them through this hellish crucible, no matter the carnage left in their wake.

Colonel Merrill and Major Ryder stood tensely on the airbase's tower balcony, binoculars trained on the empty sky. The squadron was overdue to return from another brutal bombing run into Germany's industrial heartland.

"They should have been back by now," Colonel Merrill remarked grimly.

"They may have diverted to secondary," Major Ryder suggested, though he sounded unconvinced.

Colonel Merrill's jaw tightened. "I don't like this. Four days in a row. I told the old man the entire Luftwaffe would be waiting," he said tersely. "We need longer range fighter coverage. These are becoming goddam suicide missions."

Just then, the ground chief called out, "Picking up B-seventeen's. One, two ... three, four, five ..."

As the specks grew nearer, Major Ryder continued counting. "Six, seven, eight, nine, ten ... eleven, twelve ... thirteen." He paused before asking apprehensively, "Is that it?"

"One more—fourteen," the ground chief reported sullenly, lowering his binoculars.

Major Ryder looked stricken. "Arrowhead Leader?" he asked, dreading the answer.

The ground chief nodded grimly. "Yes."

Colonel Merrill clenched his fists, cursing under his breath. "Goddam, how many did we send up, Rich?" he demanded tersely.

Head bowed, Major Ryder muttered, "Nineteen."

Colonel Merrill stood frozen, exhaling slowly as the horrific extent of their losses sunk in. "God help us," he uttered bitterly. "I'm headed back. Have Murph come see me before debriefing."

Turning briskly, the colonel departed, emotions churning inside him. Nearly a third of their planes and crews were now charred wreckage scattered across the French countryside. And those poor bastards they'd be sending up tomorrow would face the same relentless meat grinder.

When would the madness end? Were any objectives truly worth this ceaseless carnage? The colonel had no answers, only a mounting sense of futility. What right did he have to keep dispatching these brave young men to their doom?

Tommy trudged wearily into Colonel Merrill's office still clad in his flight suit, the mission's trauma still clinging to him. The colonel sat hunched over his desk, head in hands. He motioned tiredly for Tommy to sit.

"Thanks for coming by, Murph," he said heavily. "Wanted to chat before we got to debriefing. The old man wants to know what happened up there."

Tommy felt rising frustration boil over. "It was open season on us. That's what happened," he retorted bitterly. "It has been for the past month. The entire stinkin' Luftwaffe is just waiting for us. Without fighter escort, we're just sitting ducks."

Seeing the colonel's pained expression, Tommy pressed on. "But you already know that. So does H.Q., but they keep sending us."

Colonel Merrill stared bleakly at the floor. "We have to slow German production. There's no way around it," he replied resignedly. "Fighter escorts will only take us so far into Germany. There's nothing we can do about it."

Tommy shook his head vehemently. "Well, at this rate, there's not gonna be a Three hundred and sixth," he argued urgently. "We've lost a hundred and ten men this week alone. Those that made it are scared for their lives. Nobody wants to go back up."

He hesitated before admitting somberly, "I don't want to go back up."

The words hung heavily between them. Both men understood the deadly pattern couldn't continue, yet they were powerless pawns of forces beyond their control.

Colonel Merrill held up his hands placatingly. "I know, Murph, I know. I've been pleading with H.Q. to give us a breather," he said wearily. "I appealed directly to the old man. They just won't listen."

Tommy's voice took on an urgent edge. "Lord Haw Haw wasn't kidding. They have every gun in Germany trained on us," he insisted vehemently. "And Steiger. That Steiger is like a one-man squadron up there. He flamed three more today ... Got Smithy."

Tommy bowed his head, the losses suddenly overwhelming him. "I really don't think I can go back up," he confessed in a pained whisper.

Colonel Merrill slowly stood and walked around to perch on the desk beside Tommy. He clasped the young pilot's shoulder, a rare intimate gesture from the normally detached commander.

"I know, son, I know," Colonel Merrill said heavily after a thoughtful pause.

"No, you don't know," Tommy retorted, voice quavering. "I can't go up there anymore." He shook his head vehemently, staring at the floor. "I've flown nineteen missions. According to statistics, I should be dead by now."

Tommy hesitated before uttering chillingly, "I have a bad feeling about number twenty."

Colonel Merrill recoiled, spooked by the fatalism. "Grounding you isn't an option," he said uneasily. "You have more four-engine time than anyone in the Eighth Air Force. You're the only one who can lead up there. There is no other option."

The colonel paused before adding heavily, "You're gonna have to saddle up again, maybe as early as tomorrow if the cloud cover breaks. I'm sorry, Murph, it has to be that way."

Tommy just sat staring numbly at his feet, the immensity of it all bearing down on him. He was utterly depleted, just a shell of a man, but come daybreak, they would again order him to fly into the mouth of hell, no matter the cost.

Flight suits did little to shield the chilling hand of death always hovering nearby. Somehow he knew his number would be up soon, though the colonel refused to accept that grim inevitability.

In the end, there was no escape. Like a lamb to slaughter, Tommy would climb back into that cockpit because duty left no other choice. He could do little but pray for a miracle to save him from the bloodstained skies of Germany.

Chapter 12

THREADS OF FATE

DORIS SAT WITH SEVERAL other women inspectors at a long wooden table, each meticulously scrutinizing completed parachutes. They worked with careful precision, knowing any overlooked flaw could spell death for the young men relying on this life-saving equipment.

In her neatly pressed white industrial coat, Doris examined every inch and seam for imperfections. Her inspector badge and ID number were prominently displayed, underscoring the enormous responsibility entrusted to her. Though seemingly minor, even tiny defects could prove lethal when hurtling earthward at terminal velocity.

After completing her inspection, Doris swiftly marked something on the chute with the red pen she always kept close at hand. Gone were Doris's days pushing paper in some dusty accounting office.

***

Rain pattered against the window as Tony Variano lay recovering in a London hospital bed. His wounded shoulder remained heavily bandaged, but his indomitable spirit was clearly on the mend. Thumbing impatiently through an Italian newspaper, Tony glanced up to see his pretty British nurse entering. Never one to miss a chance at flirtation, he flashed his most charming grin." One stinkin' cigarette. That's all I'm asking for," Tony cajoled, giving her his most winsome look.

The nurse was having none of it. "Sorry, it's against regulations," she replied crisply.

"You Brits, always so proper," Tony scoffed. "Wish they had shipped me to Sicily to get patched up. I'd have me a smoke, a glass o' *vino*, a little smoochie smooch." He winked playfully.

The nurse crossed her arms, suppressing a smile. "You know what the problem is with you Americans?" she asked archly.

"We're too shy? Too quiet? Too handsome?" Tony guessed innocently.

Her eyes flashed with amusement, but the nurse kept her expression stern. "You Americans are OVERpaid, you're OVERsexed, and you're OVER HERE!" she declared in mock indignation.

Tony flashed his most roguish grin. "Well ... the problem with you Brits is that You're UNDERpaid,

UNDERsexed, and UNDER Eisenhower!" he shot back cheekily.

Just then Robert Hickman popped his head in the doorway. "I hope I'm not interrupting anything," Robert quipped.

The nurse huffed. "Not at all. I'm through with this patient," she declared before exiting.

Robert chuckled and approached Tony's bedside. "I asked for Benito Mussolini's room, and the clerk sent me here," he joked.

Tony's face lit up in surprise. "Hey, if it isn't the Hickman with one N, not to be confused with the Krauts," he exclaimed. "You're a long way from Connecticut, kid."

"So are you, Tony," Robert replied, smiling. "I've been seeing in the newsreels and papers that you're some kind of one-man wrecking crew, so I thought I'd see for myself."

Robert's expression turned solemn. "I'm sorry about Joe. Have you guys heard anything?"

Tony's playful demeanor faded instantly. He mutely shook his head, pain shadowing his face. The wound of that loss would not easily heal.

"Nothing," he said heavily. "The Navy doesn't know a thing. My parents go to Mass every day. We're praying the Japs fished him out and put him in a decent prison camp somewhere."

Trying to sound upbeat, Robert replied, "I thought you'd be stateside by now. Didn't they put you up for the Medal of Honor?"

But Tony shook his head dismissively. "They wanted to send me home and do that war bond nonsense, that I'm some kind of hero, but I says no way," he explained. "I need to get back with my unit, they're bogged down at Anzio. You know that's where we're from?"

Tony's voice became urgent. "No way I'm sitting this one out. I've been trying to get them to release me, but no dice. I told them I only need one good arm to fight the Jerrys."

Leaning forward eagerly, he added in a low voice, "Hey, you can actually help me out."

Robert was taken aback. "How?" he asked uncertainly.

"The Brits have a transport ship headed to Sicily tonight. I have a buddy who can sneak me on, but I have to be at the docks by midnight," Tony explained hurriedly. "You need to help me bust out of here."

Robert looked back, astonished. "Are you serious?"

"Of course I'm serious!" Tony insisted. "I gotta get to Anzio!"

Seeing Robert's reluctance, he continued persuasively, "Look, I scoped this place out. There's the main entrance, and then there's a side entrance for emergencies. It's usually quiet. Give me five minutes to get my stuff, then make a ruckus about how I was headed to the front to bust out."

Tony's eyes glinted eagerly. "All I need is a distraction. I got it from there."

Robert hesitated before relenting with a chuckle. "Okay, if that's what you want." He added jokingly, "Maybe I can sing and distract them."

Tony clasped Robert's arm gratefully. "You told me once you're not a singer, you're a fighter," he said solemnly. "I know you boys are gonna get your chance soon. God be with you all."

Robert gave a resolute nod and exited to create the diversion. Though the risky jailbreak gave him pause, he understood Tony's burning need to rejoin his band of brothers. Some duties outweighed even life itself.

***

Sal beamed with relief and pride as the B-24 dubbed "Coral Grable" taxied to a stop on the dusty South Pacific runway. As the cheerful crew clambered out, Captain Cheech Cavallo gave the aircraft's flank an affectionate pat.

"She treated us well," Cheech remarked, smiling. "Thirty missions. Sal, I think we were the only ones for all thirty."

"You deserve a medal, skipper," quipped the co-pilot. "That's a lot of Sal you had to put up with." Chuckles rippled through the group.

Cheech shot Sal a wry grin. "Let's just say I got a lifetime's worth of Sinatra out of the way," he joked, eliciting more laughter.

But Sal took the ribbing in stride. "I still have more!" he insisted breezily. "You'll have to catch my act tonight after mess. Or at the Paramount after the war."

Cheech's expression turned wistful. "I'll take a rain check on that, Caruso," he said warmly. "But I gotta say, I'm gonna miss flying with you. I'm shippin' out to the States tomorrow, gonna be test piloting some new aircraft."

"What about you, Sal?" asked the co-pilot. "What's next?"

Sal squared his shoulders importantly. "I think they have me training new navigators stateside," he reported. Then his eyes lit up enthusiastically. "What they should do is send me on a war bond tour! I'll get the folks to fork over their cash!"

The bombardier couldn't resist quipping, "They should send you to Europe for another thirty!" Laughter rippled through the group again.

But Sal just grinned, undaunted. Though unsure what awaited stateside, he had survived the deadly crucible through equal parts talent and levity. If his gifts could now serve on the home front, he would enthusiastically step up once more.

With his band of brothers soon scattering, Sal felt immensely grateful for the bonds forged aloft over blood-stained Pacific islands. Their shared courage under fire linked them for life. Whatever challenges lay ahead, Sal would face them buoyed by the lighthearted strength drawn from comrades in arms.

***

Rain drummed relentlessly on the canvas as Robert sat writing by dim lantern light. The world beyond his tent was a cold, sodden blur for months on end now. Home seemed a lifetime away.

"It seems like it's been raining for three months straight," he wrote. "I've almost forgotten what the sun looks like. The guys are jealous of me 'cause I get the most mail from home. I read and reread all your letters, and then sleep with them next to me. I try to imagine you and Maggie and Mom, like playing a film in my head. The movie doesn't have much of a plot, but the most beautiful stars!"

Robert's pen hesitated, thinking of his family so far away. "You know, I'm not a particularly religious person, but I find myself praying quite a bit," he continued. "Not in church or anything, just whenever I have a moment alone with my thoughts. I don't ask God to look over my shoulder, nothing like that. I ask God to look after you, Maggie and Mom should anything happen to me."

The words poured forth in a rush now. "I've enclosed a letter to Maggie, please read it to her when she's old enough to understand. These boys are ready to do their duty. I'm proud to serve alongside them. I remember it like yesterday, begging my Mom to sign the paper and let me do my part. Soon I'll be doing my part. Love Always, Your Robert."

Carefully folding the precious pages, Robert tucked them into his shirt pocket to be mailed come daylight. Though oceans and armies stood between them, he clung to his family through ink and memory. They were etched on his weary heart, awaiting the day he could hold them once more.

***

Izzy's heart leapt when she opened the front door to find a Navy officer standing there. Could this mean news of beloved Joe at long last?

"Good afternoon, young lady," the officer greeted her politely. "Are your parents home?"

"Yes!" Izzy exclaimed, barely containing her excitement. "Maria, go get Papa and Mama!" Her sister raced upstairs to fetch them.

"Are you with the Army?" Izzy asked eagerly while they waited.

"No, I'm with the United States Navy," the officer replied.

Izzy could scarcely breathe. "I had a broth— I have a brother in the Navy. My brother Joe," she explained hurriedly. "Have you found him?"

Before the officer could respond, Izzy's parents came rushing down. As they approached the visitor, Izzy hovered anxiously. This had to be about Joe, she told herself. After so many torturous months of uncertainty, surely word had finally come.

With barely contained hope, Izzy clasped her hands and offered up a silent prayer. She had to believe her beloved brother was still out there somewhere, just waiting to come home.

"Mr. and Mrs. Variano?" the officer began solemnly.

"Si," replied Giuseppe apprehensively.

The officer's grave expression softened into a smile. "I'm here with good news," he announced warmly. "Allied forces recently recaptured Nissan Island, part of Papua New Guinea. The Japanese were holding prisoners of war there, mostly from sunken Navy vessels. Your son Joseph was among those still alive."

Izzy gasped, scarcely allowing herself to believe it.

"He was in rough shape and is being transported to Hawaii," the officer continued. "He should make a full recovery."

Giuseppe turned to Izzy in confusion. "What is he saying?" he asked in Italian.

"Papa, Papa, Joe is alive!" Izzy cried ecstatically in Italian, jumping up and down. "Joe is alive!"

Her stunned father turned to the officer for confirmation. Overcome, her mother collapsed into his arms. Even reserved Giuseppe had tears glistening in his eyes.

Maria, who seemed like she'd been holding her breath this entire time, threw her arms around the startled officer with an elated squeal. The officer graciously returned her enthusiastic hug.

Joyful sobs mingled with laughter filled the Variano home. Their beloved Joe had beat the odds and was coming back to them. After countless prayers, their faith was finally rewarded.

THAT'S HOW IT GOES

Chapter 13

FINAL MISSION

SAL ENTERED THE BRIEFING ROOM, slightly puzzled about why he had been summoned. A lieutenant colonel greeted him briskly by a large map of the Pacific covering one wall.

"Thank you for stopping by, Variano," the officer began, lighting up a cigarette. "I want to discuss something before you ship out to Hawaii. Confidentially, in the next two weeks, we'll be receiving our first shipments of a new bomber, the B-29, at our base at Guadalcanal. We're calling it the Superfortress."

Sal's interest was piqued as the colonel continued. "It'll be the most sophisticated bomber in our fleet. Pressurized cabins, remote controlled turrets, a much higher operational ceiling."

He paused before adding meaningfully, "We'll be able to make long range bombing runs on the Japanese homeland, incapacitate their factories."

Mind racing, Sal just nodded mutely. He wasn't sure where this briefing was headed, but the top-secret information hinted at an important mission ahead.

Seeing the colonel's expectant look, Sal replied cautiously, "Yes, sir." He would hear the officer out before speculating further. But gears were already turning over what role he might play with this formidable new aircraft.

"The B-29 is a good plane but frankly hasn't been tested as much as we'd like," the colonel explained. "We need combat-hardened pilots and navigators with four-engine experience on the first run so we know what we've got with this bird."

He gave Sal an appraising look. "Your skipper speaks highly of you."

Putting out his cigarette, the colonel added pointedly, "Look, you can turn down this assignment. You've hit the magic number. I just need you on the initial run. After that, we'll cut you loose. You can rest up in Hawaii before heading to the States."

An awkward silence followed as Sal processed the request. Though exhausted, he understood the vital need to properly vet this long-range bomber. And he wouldn't abandon his brothers on the eve of their victory lap.

"Sure, count me in," Sal finally agreed, mustering his trademark breezy grin. "The Hula Honeys can wait a bit more."

The colonel looked immensely relieved. "You're doing your country a great service, son," he said earnestly, shaking Sal's hand. "We'll make sure you get stateside soon enough."

Sal nodded crisply, hoping the older man's assurances proved true. He would gladly play his part ushering in this bold new aircraft built to carry the war right to Japan's doorstep. Just one more mission, he told himself. One more song for the boys, then home to his long-delayed dreams.

***

The tropical sun beat down on the remote Papua New Guinea airstrip as Nurse Drury helped a stream of emaciated prisoners of war aboard a medical transport plane. After enduring months of horrific captivity, these men were finally freed when Allied forces recaptured Nissan Island.

Nurse Drury extended a steadying hand to one unsteady sailor. "Can I help you on?" she asked gently.

The ghostly man looked back incredulously, as if unsure this rescue was real. "I ... I—thank you," he stammered in a raspy voice. "We didn't know if anyone—" Overcome by emotion, he struggled to speak further.

Nurse Drury's heart ached at the trauma these men had endured. "We're going to take good care of you all. Promise," she assured him soothingly.

Clutching her hand desperately, the sailor asked in confusion, "Where are we?"

"You're okay now," Nurse Drury replied. "We're going to the naval hospital at Guadalcanal. We're gonna get you cleaned up and healthy, sailor. You're going home."

Tears streamed down the man's gaunt face. "We knew you were coming back for us," he choked out. "We just knew."

With immense tenderness, Nurse Drury helped him board the transport. A line of fellow survivors awaited her care. Though the road ahead was long, she vowed these men would find healing in body and spirit. Their unimaginable sacrifice deserved nothing less.

***

The tranquil blue sky was violently shattered by bursts of flak and streaks of machine gun fire as the battered B-17 formation continued its perilous push over Germany. Swarming enemy fighters harassed the bombers relentlessly, preying on any lagging aircraft.

One B-17 rapidly lost altitude, belching smoke from an engine as it fell behind the main group. The vicious fighters descended upon the crippled plane, peppering it mercilessly with rounds, its familiar "Lucky Charm" nose art visible on the mangled flank.

Inside, Tommy wrestled to keep the battered B-17 airborne as enemy fighters swarmed like hornets outside. The cockpit instruments had gone haywire and his co-pilot slumped cold and motionless in the seat beside him.

"Status of crew?" Tommy shouted desperately into the radio. "Status? Who's back there?" Only ominous silence answered.

The bombardier's panicked voice finally crackled over the speaker. "Both gunners are dead, Murph! Navigator bleeding heavily. I've been hit but okay."

Tommy's gut clenched, but he tried staying focused on the controls. "We're listing!" he yelled back tersely. "Trying to get power to right-most engine."

The bombardier reported urgently amidst pinging bullets, "Electrical is on fire back here! Doing my best to put it out."

Ice coursed through Tommy's veins. They were sitting ducks, hemorrhaging men and altitude. But he couldn't give up yet. Gritting his teeth, he pulled back desperately on the yoke, willing the stricken bomber to stay aloft.

Glancing out the window through the smoke, Tommy glimpsed the distant specks that were the intact formation, now far out of reach. No savior awaited. He was utterly alone guiding his men to their likely deaths.

"I'm okay but out of ammo," the ball-turret gunner reported urgently over the radio. "Bandit closing, four o'clock!"

Heart lurching, Tommy glimpsed the familiar markings on the approaching fighter—it was German ace Friedrich Steiger, back to feast once more. The Lucky Charm's luck had just run out.

Time seemed to slow as Steiger pulled alongside, peering into the bomber's burning interior. Through the smoke-filled plexiglass, he glimpsed a nightmarish scene of carnage and desperation.

The dead crew members lay broken and bloodied, while a gravely wounded comrade fruitlessly tried extinguishing the electrical fire consuming the rear. Acrid black smoke billowed through the cabin past the terrified young ball turret gunner, trapped helplessly in his glass bubble.

The bomber was utterly crippled and defenseless, its remaining crew powerlessly awaiting the hunter's fatal strike. Steiger's finger rested lightly on the machine gun trigger, ready to add to his chilling tally of kills. Their eyes briefly locked, and Tommy braced for the end, knowing there was nothing he could do.

But to his disbelief, Steiger gave a slight head shake and veered away without firing. The cold-blooded killer had just spared them. Tommy's eyes flooded with stunned gratitude.

Somehow the bomber stayed aloft as Steiger flew protectively alongside, blocking other fighters from finishing them off. The deadly foe had shown inexplicable mercy, allowing the "Lucky Charm" to limp westward out of enemy airspace.

Its crew decimated, the bomber would never fly again. But by some miracle, Tommy had survived to see another day. Steiger had spared his crippled prey for reasons only he knew.

Gazing at the German ace through tear-filled eyes, Tommy offered up a silent prayer of thanks. They were enemies forced together by duty yet bonded by honor in that moment miles above earthly conflicts.

Two pilots had glimpsed their common humanity amidst the inhumane machinery of war. Though Tommy knew his flying days were likely over, today he would live because mercy triumphed over hate.

Tommy slogged wearily across the tarmac with his ball-turret gunner, the battered "Lucky Charm" smoking behind them on the runway. Nearby, an ambulance raced away.

Approaching Colonel Merrill's Jeep, they were met with shocked expressions. "The rest of the planes landed twenty-five minutes ago," the colonel exclaimed incredulously. "We assumed you bailed or went down. How did you make it back?!?"

Tommy just shook his head grimly. "Lucky, I guess," he muttered. "It wasn't our time. But I'll be writing letters tonight."

The excited ball-turret gunner jumped in. "You're not gonna believe what happened up there, Colonel! We were just sitting ducks and Stei—"

Tommy silenced him with a sharp look and terse head shake. "Nothing happened up there," he interjected pointedly. "The crew muscled through it. We made it back."

The gunner clammed up as they climbed into the Jeep. As they drove off, Tommy kept his gaze fixed straight ahead. The true story of their salvation was sealed behind his lips. He had peered into the enemy's humanity, but the world saw only black and white.

The noble act of one could not undo the evils of many, but Steiger had allowed Tommy to live another day. For that precious gift, Tommy vowed eternal silence.

***

Robert stood frozen in awed reverence as General Eisenhower, Supreme Allied Commander, addressed the paratroopers on the eve of D-Day, June 5th, 1944.

"Men, I stopped by to tell you that the eyes of the world will be on you tomorrow," Eisenhower declared solemnly. "The hope and prayers of liberty-loving people everywhere will be with you."

He swept his gaze over the jumpers' expectant faces. "You will help bring about the destruction of the German war machine, the end of Nazi tyranny over the oppressed peoples of Europe."

Eisenhower's tone turned grave. "Boys, it won't be easy. Your enemy is well trained, well equipped and battle-hardened." Then he smiled reassuringly. "But I have full confidence in your courage, devotion to duty and skill in battle, and I know God will be with you."

As one, the airborne troops roared back "AIRBORNE!" The sound thundered through the countryside. Robert's chest swelled with devotion and pride.

As Supreme Allied Commander Eisenhower walked down the line of paratroopers, he asked one young private, "Son, where are you from?"

"Wichita, Kansas, sir!" the private responded proudly.

"I was raised in Abilene, not far from there," Eisenhower remarked. "God be with you, son."

Moving on, he shook hands with the next jumper. "And you?" Eisenhower asked.

"From Potomac, Maryland, sir!" the private responded.

"They feeding you well here?" Eisenhower inquired lightheartedly.

"We can use some Maryland crabs, sir!" drawing chuckles from the men.

Further down, Eisenhower came to Robert Hickman and shook his hand. "What about you, son? You need anything from home?" he asked sincerely.

"No, sir. Can't wait to see my wife and baby," Robert replied.

Eisenhower smiled warmly. "I hope your parents are proud. Your country is," he said.

"Mom is working for Uncle Sam," Robert shared. "I'm proud of her."

Eisenhower nodded approvingly. "Godspeed, son. May His grace shine on you tomorrow," he offered before moving on.

Robert was incredibly moved to speak one-on-one with the legendary general. Eisenhower's inspiring words would stay with him as he embarked on this monumental mission to liberate Europe. Every paratrooper knew the gravity of what they faced and how much was at stake. But they had trained relentlessly for this very moment and did not shrink from their duty.

Robert stood a little taller, buoyed by Eisenhower's confidence in them. Though peril awaited, he took comfort knowing the hopes and prayers of the free world would be with the airborne troops come dawn. They would give their all.

THAT'S HOW IT GOES

Chapter 14

THE LONGEST NIGHT

SAL STRODE ACROSS the tarmac with his new B-29 bomber crew toward the gleaming Superfortress awaiting them. Noting the aircraft's bare fuselage, he called out to the pilot, "You need some nose art on this bird, skipper. Watcha gonna call her?"

The handsome pilot flashed a grin. "I'm thinking about naming her 'Hollywood,'" he revealed.

Sal gave him a quizzical look. "That don't sound much like a woman's name," he remarked dubiously.

"He's naming it after himself," the chuckling co-pilot explained. "That's what we call him, Hollywood Heyda. 'Cause he's too handsome not to be in the movies!"

The pilot posed theatrically as if on a movie poster. "It's true, my friend," he proclaimed in his deepest voice. "The camera loves me!"

Sal laughed, immediately liking this crew's breezy camaraderie. As they climbed aboard, he knew fitting in would be no trouble. Their lighthearted spirits reminded him of his very first crew back in flight school, before the heavy toll of war had weighed down their souls.

Maybe, Sal thought to himself, just maybe he could rediscover that youthful zeal on this Superfortress mission. With competent veterans at his side once more, he looked forward to completing his service on a high note.

***

In his tent, Robert meticulously inspected his parachute and gear alongside three other jumpers, just hours from boarding the C-47s headed for Normandy. The atmosphere was tense with focus.

"Man, I'm glad I paid attention in jump school on packing chutes," one private remarked tersely. "We get one shot at this."

The others murmured solemn agreement. Robert carefully ran his hands along each seam and strap, mentally envisioning an ideal landing on French soil come dawn. Unexpectedly, he noticed something on the parachute material.

"I know my chute is gonna work," Robert muttered to nobody in particular.

"What?" one of the puzzled jumpers asked.

"My chute," Robert repeated, looking up. "I know it's gonna take care of me."

The private eyed Robert strangely. "What are you talking about?" he asked, irritation edging his voice.

"The chutes ... they're made down the street from my house, in Norwalk," Robert explained. "Used to bike past that plant every day."

He rubbed the smooth material between his fingers, lost in bittersweet memories.

"Yeah, so?" one of the puzzled jumpers remarked impatiently.

"The Paramount Parachute Company," Robert clarified, looking up.

The private just shrugged. "They gotta be made somewhere," he replied dismissively.

Robert persisted, voice growing emotional. "My mom works there, as an inspector."

"Hooray for Mom," the exasperated jumper retorted sarcastically.

But Robert was transfixed, slowly lowering the canopy to reveal bold red initials—DCH.

"And her initials are on my chute," he uttered, voice cracking.

The others gathered around in astonishment as Robert reverently traced the letters with his finger. His beloved mother had inspected this very parachute, unwittingly safeguarding her only child.

Robert was overwhelmed by the realization. However tomorrow unfolded, he would leap into the darkness wrapped in her loving protection once more. Together, they would defy the pull of gravity to see him safely home.

***

Sal gripped his navigation table as the Superfortress neared the bombing target, buffeted by flak bursts and machine gun fire. Hollywood Heyda's voice crackled over the radio. "Over target. Plane is yours, bombardier."

"Roger that. Bombs away," the bombardier confirmed tersely. Sal braced himself as the aircraft lurched upward, freed of its deadly payload.

"Your plane, Captain," the bombardier reported once clear.

"Roger that," Heyda responded. "Angel One to all crews, let's head for home. Set course two-three-five."

But their escape was blocked. "Zekes at ten o'clock!" the co-pilot yelled.

"Evasive maneuvers!" Heyda ordered urgently. The bomber banked hard, its gunners returning fire at the swarming Japanese Zeros.

Amidst the chaos, the bombardier's panicked shout knifed through Sal. "Sal's been hit!"

Sal looked down to see blood rapidly soaking his uniform.

"Go back there!" Heyda ordered the co-pilot urgently. The man raced to Sal's aid, finding him now slumped over and bleeding heavily from the abdomen. Sal was still conscious, but ghostly pale.

The co-pilot quickly applied pressure to the wound. "Hang in there, Sal," he urged. "We're headed back to Guadal."

Through gritted teeth, Sal clasped his hand tightly. "Okay. Stay with me," he implored weakly.

Trying to keep Sal's spirits up, the co-pilot joked, "I will. Just promise me no singing."

Sal managed a pained chuckle before his expression turned serious once more. "Stay with me," he repeated, fresh blood blooming across the bandages.

The co-pilot nodded, holding Sal's gaze. "I'm right here, buddy. And I'm not going anywhere," he vowed.

Sal focused on the man's face, drawing comfort from his steadying presence as icy shock crept through his veins. He had endured so much to reach this final mission, only to face his greatest trial now aloft over the Pacific. But he would not face it alone. His crew was with him.

The Superfortress roared to a stop on Guadalcanal's runway, its weary crew clambering out. Medics rushed forward as two men bore the gravely wounded Sal Variano on a stretcher, his face ashen beneath blood-soaked bandages.

"We can't stop the bleeding!" the frantic co-pilot cried. "He's fading in and out. He needs blood!"

Among the medics was none other than Nurse Grace Drury. Seeing Sal's limp form, utter anguish twisted her face. This was the playful boy who had flirted so harmlessly back home. Now he hovered at death's door after bravely answering duty's call.

With infinite tenderness, Grace took Sal's cold hand in hers as the men lowered him to the tarmac. Tears streamed down her cheeks as she willed him to open his eyes once more.

Mustering her composure, Grace choked out, "Of all the gin joints in all the towns ..."

Hearing the familiar words, the ghost of a smile graced Sal's ashen face. "I—I ... saw—you," he whispered almost inaudibly.

"Where?" Grace implored, leaning close to catch his fading words.

"Hawaii ..." Sal repeated distantly, eyes fluttering. "I'm tired."

Grace clasped his hand tighter, willing him to stay. "Golden voice that night," she whispered yearningly. "Golden voice."

But Sal's strength was spent. "Tired," he murmured, eyes closing as consciousness slipped from his grasp.

"You can't sleep. Hang on," Grace pleaded through anguished sobs. She could not let him go, not like this.

With his last ounce of breath, Sal softly crooned a ghostly refrain: "That's how it goes ..."

The song that had bound their fate now marked its end. Grace wept bitterly, clutching Sal's lifeless hand to her cheek. His melody was silenced, his light extinguished.

But the memory of that golden USO night and the first time she heard Sal sing at the Army recruitment office would stay locked in her heart, untarnished by the war's cruel toll. Though muted now, Sal's voice would forever echo in her soul. That's how it goes.

EPILOGUE

THE HORRORS OF WAR inevitably faded into memory as life resumed its hopeful rhythm. Tony Variano was awarded the Medal of Honor by President Truman himself, making him the second most decorated soldier of World War II. Beaming proudly alongside Tony that day were his English nurse bride and the entire Variano clan, including brother Joe, whose life was spared by a miracle. Tony went on to coach football for 37 years, molding generations of young men.

Though opportunities abounded, Nurse Grace Drury continued serving her country, caring for the wounded in Korea and Vietnam and achieving the rank of colonel. She never wed, keeping close company instead with music and treasured memories that time could not diminish.

Tommy Murphy built a successful business as a general contractor and became a patron of the arts after surviving twenty-five deadly bombing missions. His son

Salvatore inherited his namesake's musical gifts, starring in school plays at the Salvatore Variano Auditorium. And in time, forgiveness brought Tommy unexpected friendship with the German ace who had spared him.

Donning his uniform one last time, Robert Hickman came home to the embrace of his stalwart mother and devoted young wife, Peggy. From his pocket he drew a swatch of parachute marked boldly with her initials—the very one that had saved his life. Doris nearly fainted at the revelation, overwhelmed by her role in protecting her only child. In time, Robert and Peggy made Manhattan home, raising three children under Doris's doting eye.

Though war's sacrifices could never be repaid, postwar life blossomed as hope triumphed over despair. Their fighting spirit lived on through generations spared global tyranny by the valiant few. The torch was passed, its light undimmed.

AUTHOR'S NOTE

This is my first attempt at fiction. I've written four books on history, one book about my daughter Mona, and now my first Novella.

It was inspired by real people and real events that I've become familiar with during the course of creating my Youtube Channel, This Date in History with Nick Ragone, which has exceeded my wildest expectations.

The channel was created on a lark one Sunday afternoon in 2023 when I was lamenting to my wife and my brother Tom about the mediocrity of history videos on Youtube. "Then start a damn channel and stop whining," was Tom's big brotherly advice. Spot on as usual.

This book is just as much his as mine. My brother Tom is the creative genius and beating heart behind our Youtube Channel. Together, we've lived and breathed the real men and women of the Greatest Generation who have helped make America so exceptional. We've been humbled to be able to tell their amazing stories and we will continue to do so. Working with Tommy on this has been the absolute blessing of a lifetime, more rewarding than anything I've ever done in my professional career. It almost makes up for him tricking me into being a Mets fan before I was old enough to know better.

As with all my previous books, this one wouldn't be possible without my loving and beautiful wife, Tyan. Like all the ideas in my head, this book would be just that—an idea—were it not for her unconditional and unwavering support. I am a lucky, lucky man.

And if you were imagining a movie while reading the book, then your imagination is working well. It was actually a movie script first – and it's a really good one for you enterprising Hollywood types – and I'm sure it'll be on the big screen someday!

This book is dedicated to the countless million men and women who have served this country so selflessly. May God bless them always.

Made in the USA
Las Vegas, NV
26 July 2024